All Flavors

A Book of Erotic Short Stories

D M Gaines

New Flavor
Books

All Flavors: A Book of Erotic Short Stories

Library of Congress Control Number: 2013937261

Editing and cover design by
Earvin Taze. Watters Jr.
ezatcreations@yahoo.com
newflavorbooksandpublishingllc.com

Revised January 2015

New Flavor Books an imprint of New Flavor Books & Publishing, LLC

New Flavor Books & Publishing, LLC
PO Box 603323
Cleveland, Ohio 44103

Books by D M Gaines

Hood to Hood: A Cleveland Story
Hood to Hood 2: Spank's Revenge
Sexual Addiction: Director's Cut
All Flavors: A Book of Erotic Short Stories
Bisexual Bliss
Hittin' Licks
Murder or Justice
Deadly Surgeon

Dedication

This book is dedicated to all of the men and women in the world, who are not afraid of seeking to fulfill their sexual fantasies and desires.

Acknowledgements

I would like to thank my son and daughter-in-law Kevin Johnson and Beverly Johnson for all of their help and support. I would like to thank my daughter Brittiny Roseberry, no matter what we go through I still love you. I would like to thank my business partner and best friend Earvin Taze Watters Jr, there is no limit to the things that we can do. I would like to thank Darrin Fears, thank you for always being a true friend from childhood until now. I would also like to thank my sister Latasha Gibson, you are my motivation whether you know it or not. I will also like to thank Veronica Thompson and Victoria Tori Johnson. And last but not least thank you to everyone that has supported me, God bless you all.

Sincerely, D. M. Gaines

Table of Contents

Flashbacks

I remember when I was young I was sent to a youth facility for joyriding in a stolen car where I was sentenced to six months. While there I was enrolled in an educational program to get my diploma.

There was a guidance counselor named Ms. Crane. She was an older lady in her late 40's or early 50's. Ms. Crane was liked by everyone from the juvies to the other staff. She had a sweet personality and was very helpful.

She was very small and petite, and had a sickly appearance, yet there were still traces of her past sexiness and a gleam in her eyes. She had no complexes and seemed oblivious to some of the things she did, like sitting with her legs open showing off how fat her pussy was or bending over straight from the hip which showed that she had a beautiful ass. Sometimes she would bend over while wearing baggy shirts with no bra, allowing a full view of her little titties with big nipples. I often wondered why she would hang around the gym and would sometime enter the boy's locker room while we were getting dressed. Sometimes she would even work the blocks doing overtime.

The shower stall was a mass one with a window so the staff could look in to make sure all was well. Whenever it was shower time Ms. Crane stayed at the window. She would even walk in the bathroom and check all of the stalls. It wasn't hard for any one that actually paid attention to see that Ms. Crane was a freak. Most people looked at her like she was naive and sickly but I saw something different. I was finally proven right when she worked overtime in our dorm on third shift one night.

I was in the restroom in the last stall with a girly magazine, plain and simple I was beating my meat. I had the magazine in a chair in front of me whacking my meat when I heard someone enter the restroom. I heard soft footsteps and I called out, "Who's there?" no one answered, so I stopped what I was doing and listened for a minute, but I didn't hear another sound.

I continued what I was doing and was getting worked up and was seconds away from ejaculating when I heard a soft muffled moan. As I began to ejaculate I heard that same soft moan. This time the moan wasn't muffled. I quickly jumped up, and there was Ms. Crane leaning on the wall with her hand in her pants.

I spoke, "Ms. Crane!" she looked up with a shocked expression on her face and quickly removed her hand from her pants. Once she composed herself she stated, "I was just making my rounds, are you okay?"

I said, "Yes ma'am, I was just using the restroom."

She said, "Well alright let me finish making my rounds you get back to your bunk." Ms. Crane turned and left out the restroom. I cleaned up and went back to my bunk.

I could not go back to sleep, all I could think about was Ms. Crane actually masturbating while watching me jack off. I thought of an excuse to go to the office.

As I made my way to the office I could see that the office lights were dim for a minute I thought she wasn't even in there, but as I got closer I could see legs up on the desk. I got to the door and it looked as if she was sleeping, she was reclined back in the chair with her eyes closed. I was debating on whether or not I wanted to disturb her sleep, when all of a sudden I heard that same moan that I had heard earlier in the restroom. I was shocked and thought to myself, "Was she really masturbating?"

I decided to take a chance, so I opened the door. She was so caught up in herself that she did not hear me enter the room. Her pants were unzipped with her hand down in them working her pussy. I instantly got hard and I pulled my dick out and began stroking it when all of a sudden Ms. Crane opened her eyes with an astonished look on her face.

She attempted to compose herself as she said, "Mr. Phillips what are you doing?"

I said, "Ms. Crane it's obvious you need tending to. First, you were masturbating while watching me in the restroom, now I find you in here doing the same thing, so I thought I would assist you."

She tried to get all serious and professional on me by saying, "Young man you're trying to get me to lose my job, and for the record you are too young."

I replied, "Cut the games, you are not going to lose your job this is between us, far as me being a kid, what you think about this?" I pointed down to my dick. She looked down and said, "Oh my! How old are you?"

"I'm 17 years old!"

"You are big for your age."

"Oh my Lord, I'm going to get myself into a world of trouble." Then she said, "Why would you want me?"

"Because you are beautiful and sexy and I have always had a thing for older women."

"You youngsters are so slick you will say anything to get what you want."

"Believe what you want to believe Ms. Crane I just want to give you the type of loving that I think you need, so please allow me to do that."

"What do you want from me?" she asked.

"Come to me and I will handle the rest." She nervously walked towards me and stopped in front of me. I reached behind her head and released the clip that held her hair in a ponytail, allowing her hair to fall down freely to her shoulders, which made her even sexier. I reached out and unbuttoned her blouse. She shivered nervously.

"Relax everything is going to be okay." I said to her.

I undid the buttons on her pants and let them fall down to her ankles and she stepped out of them. I told Ms. Crane to turn around for me. When she turned around I unhooked the clasp on her bra and removed it. I took my arms and hooked them under hers and reached up and cuffed both of her breasts and massaged them gently. She let out a sigh as she leaned back against my chest.

I lifted her hair up and proceeded to nibble on her ear and plant gentle kisses on her neck. She continued to let out soft moans. I then took both of my hands to help her out of her panties. I had her turn back towards me and I knelt in front of her. I used both of my hands to separate her pussy lips so that her clit was exposed, it was poking out erect.

I let my mouth engulf her whole pussy until my tongue entered her pussy. This caused her legs to shake violently that I thought she would fall. She put both of her hands on the top of my head for support.

I did every trick I knew from blowing on her clit, using two fingers to rub her pussy to nibbling on it. She let out a high streak and held her head back and started cumming. Her cum dripped down the corners of my mouth.

After Ms. Crane regained her composure she said, "I never would of have thought that a boy of your age could do something like that, where did you learn that?"

"I have been around and its some more things that I want to show you." I said as I stood up.

"Turn around and put your hands on the desk." I told her and she obliged. I used my hands to get her in the perfect position. I bent her over and arched her back. I used one of my legs to part her legs further apart. Then I took both of my hands used my thumbs to separate her ass cheeks.

I was amazed that Ms. Crane had a nice firm ass for her age. Her pussy looked so beautiful from the back. I guided my dick into her and she was super tight and super wet. Her pussy felt so good it made me moan.

I watched my dick go in and out of Ms. Crane's pussy. I removed my hands from her ass and put them on her waist, this gave me a better grip and I long dicked her. I picked up the pace fucking her a little harder. Because of how frail she was and everyone saying that she was sick, I felt that I had to be gentle with her.

Ms. Crane gave me a hell of a surprise when she initiated fucking me back. She gyrated her hips and was meeting my thrust, and she was doing it with force. Ms. Crane bucked and shook her head wildly, which had her hair flying everywhere. She was making all kinds of noises. It was like she was possessed.

Here it was, I was trying to be gentle and she was acting like a wild beast. I thought I better step it up, so I grabbed her hair wrapped it around my fist and pulled her head back and started pounding the hell out of her.

I was fucking her so hard that the desk was shaking along with her ass cheeks and her titties. It was unbelievable, the more intense I fucked her the more intense she fucked back.

Ms. Crane was trying to say something but she couldn't get the words out. She was convulsing and her body started to spasm, which let me know that she was cumming again.

I felt the tension rise in my nuts and knew that I was about to cum as well. I put my left foot up on the desk and fucked her fiercely. Ms. Crane broke my spell when she said, "Put it in my mouth! Put it in my mouth!" I was at the point where I was not going to be able to stop myself from cumming so I pulled out of her and quickly grabbed my dick with both of my hands.

She turned and knelt down and as soon as my dick got to her mouth and I released my grip I started skeeting. The first squirt hit her between her eyes and nose and the second one, on her lips. She had me in her mouth sucking me dry. I looked down and saw that her hair was hanging down in front of her face and she was looking like a porno star.

ꆠ

I am a grown man now and as I look back I do not think that anyone that knew Ms. Crane would believe this story. She had many people fooled, even me. I learned that everything isn't as it seem. Who would have thought that a frail, sickly looking middle aged lady could be such a freak.

๑

After we finished that night she made me promise to never tell a sole and I never did. The day before I left she called me into her office. She told me that I was a special young man and that I was going to make some young lady very happy, then she gave me a blowjob and sent me back to the dorm.

That's a memory that I will never forget.

Two Is Better Than One

Mike was in his bedroom standing before the mirror, making sure that he had everything together. That night was to be the big night for him to score with Monica. They had been dating for almost two months and the furthest he had gotten with her was to finger fuck her.

Mike was hyped, because Monica promised him that they would go all the way that night, so he felt that he had to look and smell his best. He did not want any errors on his part. After he made sure that he had everything right he picked up his car keys and headed for the door.

𝄞

Monica was just getting out of the shower, freshening up after a long day at work. She was getting ready for Mike's arrival. She promised that night he could get some pussy. She hadn't fucked in a while and was looking forward to getting some good dick.

As she slid into her panties her doorbell rang, she thought to herself, "Damn he early, he couldn't wait to get this pussy!"

Without putting on anything, she went to answer the door. Monica opened the door and was surprised to see her best friend Neicy. Neicy had been gone away to college for the past three years. Monica said, "Hey girl what's up?" as she reached out to give her a hug.

Neicy said, "I just flew in, I'm only here for the weekend so I thought that I would drop by to see you." Monica stepped back and let Neicy come all the way in so that she could close the door.

Neicy looked at Monica fully as she stood there in only her panties. Neicy gave a devilish smile then said, "I'm glad I dropped by." Monica picked up on her comment but ignored it and asked, "So where are you staying?"

"Girl I'm getting a hotel room, unless you gone offer to let me stay with you?" she asked as she once again looked Monica up and down with a gleam in her eyes. Monica reflected back to the times they had sexually experimented with each other and decided that it would be okay for her to stay, but she had to let her know about Mike.

She said, "Of course you can stay here but I have a date coming over too, so you go have to sleep on the couch." Neicy said, "It's cool, which way are you going though?"

"What do you mean which way I'm going?" she asked.

"Is your date with a man or woman?"

"Girl, you are tripping, it's a man. You the only girl that I ever got down with like that."

"Yeah I better be the only one! I'm just playing girl, it's cool I will stay out of the way." Neicy said.

"Okay then girl, I am about to go finish getting ready."

ฦ

As Mike headed towards Monica's house, he decided to call and let her know that he was on his way. He pulled out his cell phone and dialed her number. she answered on the second ring.

"Hey what are you doing?"

"I just got through talking with my best friend, who just came into town." Mike's heart instantly dropped. All he saw was his shot at fucking Monica going out the window. With more attitude than he wanted to display, Mike said, "You know I'm on my way over right now, is everything still as planned?"

"Boy ain't nothing changed. She staying here for the weekend, but she knows to stay out of the way." Monica told him. Mike let out a sigh of relief and said, "Cool I will be there in about a half an hour." and hung up.

After Monica finished getting ready she went back downstairs. Neicy was sitting on the couch. She looked up and said, "So who is this guy, and how long have y'all been dating?"

"It's been two months and his name is Mike." Monica answered.

"So have y'all fucked yet?" Neicy asked.

"Girl you crazy, why you ask me something like that?" asked Monica.

"I want to know what he is working with. I might want to join y'all like old times." Neicy told her.

Monica said, "Girl I ain't even fucked him yet. I don't even know if he is into that type of stuff, plus I ain't on that anymore!"

"Girl, you always acting funny, you go always be a freak you need to come out of the closet."

Neicy said, "Girl I like him I don't want him looking at me like I'm some type of slut!"

Neicy got hyped, "Bitch! Every man's fantasy is to be with two women that will blow his mind."

Monica sighed and said, "Girl you always pushing me to do some freaky shit."

"Bitch!"

"I don't be pushing you to do shit"

"You a bigger freak than me just sneaky."

"Shit! I would be sleep and wake up to you sucking the shit out of this pussy!" Neicy said with a laugh.

"Yeah whatever," said Monica.

Neicy said, "I got an idea we can have some drinks, play a few games and see where things go."

Monica said, "Girl what type of games?"

Neicy replied, "Some strip poker or truth or dare."

"Bitch! You crazy he go bug out on our asses."

"Well we go see how he is live or a cornball." stated Neicy.

Monica said, "Well he is on his way, so I will get the drinks and the cards out."

"Let me get my bags out of the car so that I can change into something more comfortable." stated Neicy.

꩜

Mike pulled up to Monica's house. He got out and rang the doorbell. Monica opened the door wearing a black mini skirt, a sheer black blouse and some come fuck me black pumps. Mike stood there looking at her intently.

Monica had to break his spell, "Boy you coming in or what?"

"Damn my fault!" Mike said as he stepped in.

"It's all good have a seat." she said. Mike sat down and got his composure back and said, "How do you want to start the night off?" Monica said, "Well since my friend is here I figured we could have a few drinks and play some cards or some other games." Mike thought to himself, "I knew it was go be some bullshit."

Just as he was about to protest the bathroom door opened and Neicy stepped out wearing nothing but a matching pink bra and panty set. Mike looked at her like damn she's a bad bitch.

Neicy stood about 5' 3" and had a beautiful caramel complexion. She had smooth skin, a pretty face with almond shaped eyes. Neicy was also built like a brick house.

She walked over and introduced herself, "Hi, I'm Neicy Monica's friend I hope that my surprise visit didn't spoil y'all plans?"

Neicy followed up by saying, "You know one time I heard an old cliché, that two is better than   one." Mike did not know how to interpret that statement. Monica spoke up by saying, "Let me get y'all some drinks. I got Jack and Hennessy."

Mike said, "I'll take some Hen."

Neicy said, "Give me a double of Jack!"

Monica went into the kitchen to make the drinks. Neicy took the opportunity to quiz Mike.

"So Mike are you spontaneous and creative?"

"It all depends on what you are talking about," Mike responded.

"I'm talking about women and living life."

Mike said, "Yeah I guess you can say that I am."

"Well that's good, because I asked Monica if you would be up for a game of strip poker or truth or dare."

Mike said, "I'm game for whatever, but you're already stripped aren't you?"

Neicy laughed and said, "The odds are already against me, it should be an easy win."

Monica came back with the drinks.

Neicy said, "Girl he cool as hell, he's down for whatever."

Mike said, "I didn't know you were live like this!"

Monica laughed and said, "Boy we haven't known each other two months yet, it's a lot you don't know about me."

Mike responded, "Well hopefully after tonight I will know a lot more."

"So what game do y'all want to play poker or truth or dare?" Neicy asked.

Mike said, "How about we play both of them, starting with strip poker."

Neicy said, "See girl I told you he was live, I like him."

They moved to the dining room table where they played strip poker. They had no idea that this was Mike's game. After three or four drinks and seven hands of poker Mike had both women completely naked. However, Monica still had on her heels.

Neicy whined, "This ain't fair, here it is we are completely naked and you're sitting there with all your clothes on."

Mike said, "Hey this was y'all idea not mine, so let's move on to the next game."

"Just like a man!" Monica said.

Mike smiled and said, "Don't worry y'all will get your turn, but for now Neicy pick one truth or dare." Neicy chose dare.

"I dare you to kiss Monica"

"Boy that ain't nothing." Neicy said

"Not on her mouth but on her pussy."

Monica blurted out, "Boy you tripping, I knew I shouldn't have played this game."

Neicy jumped in, "It's cool girl let's show this nigga how real bitches get down. Sit on the chair and put your legs over the arms." Monica sat down in the chair and put her legs over the sides leaving her pussy open for all to see.

Neicy knelt down in front of her. She took her thumbs and forefingers to spread her pussy lips even more, so that her clit was exposed. She put her mouth down there and blew on her clit. Monica let out a moan and said, "Girl just kiss it and get it over with."

Neicy said, "Girl you know that ain't happening. I'm about to do more than kiss this pussy." With that being said she flicked her tongue over Monica's clit sending shivers through Monica. Then she started gently nibbling and sucking on it. Monica held her head back and gripped the side arms of the chair.

Mike sat in amazement, he did not expect any of what was happening, but he was glad. The only time he had been with two women was when he was with two strawberries. So he was going to make sure that this was going to be one of the best moments of his life.

He sat taking in the show. It was as if they had forgotten all about him. They were so caught up. Neicy was now using two fingers on her right hand to fuck her. Monica's pussy was puffy and her clit was swollen. Neicy used two fingers on her left hand to rub her clit in a circular motion. With the two fingers on the other hand she picked up her rhythm. Monica started shaking her head back and forth saying, "Damn Neicy shit I'm cumming!" This caused Neicy to speed up her rhythm.

She said, "That's it bitch cum for momma, cum for me baby!"

Monica came, and cum ran out of her pussy and coated Neicy's fingers. Neicy removed her fingers from Monica's pussy and put them in her mouth and sucked all the juices off. They were still oblivious to Mike's presence until they heard some hands clapping.

They turned to Mike who said, "Good show ladies, but the game must go on. So which one of you ladies would like to go next?"

Neicy said, "I will!" she directed her challenge to Mike, who picked truth. Neicy asked, "Are you holding?"

Mike said, "Of course!"

"There is only one way to find out if you are telling the truth." Neicy replied.

"I dare you to strip off your clothes." Mike smiled and said not a problem. He quickly started to undress. In seconds he was down to nothing but his socks. Monica and Neicy appraised him from head to toe and liked what they saw. Mike stood there proud with his hands on his hips and legs slightly spread.

Neicy said, "Damn girl look at his dick it's big as hell!"

Monica chimed in, "Shit I ain't never seen no balls that big that hang like that. Every time he fucks a bitch she must get pregnant."

"You ain't even hard yet, are you?" Neicy asked.

Mike said, "Nope, but if we get back to the game I might get there."

It was now Monica's turn and she dared Neicy to suck his dick. Neicy said, "I will do what I can!" Neicy dropped to her knees in front of Mike. She reached out to Mike with both hands.

One went to his dick and the other went to his balls. She was amazed at the weight of them and her pussy instantly became wet. She started stroking his dick, feeling it pulsate and grow bigger in her hands. It grew at least three more inches. Mike grabbed her head and guided it until his dick was at the entrance of her mouth. He told her, "Don't get scared on me baby girl, you can handle it."

Neicy responded, "I ain't never scared." Then she opened her mouth and took him in. First she just worked the head, then she started to take him in deeper. She put both of her hands on the base of his dick and started making love to it with her mouth with her eyes closed.

She began making slurping sounds and saliva was dripping out the corners of her mouth. Mike had his eyes closed enjoying the sensation. Suddenly, he felt another warm sensation on his balls. He opened his eyes and looked down and there was Monica kneeling right next to Neicy sucking on his balls. Mike was in heaven, he felt like the luckiest man in the world. Mike got their attention by saying, "I like how y'all work as a team, but we got to change up. I got to get my dick in some pussy."

Monica said, "Well it better be me, this was supposed to be our night."

"Don't worry, Neicy wanted to know if I was creative. Check this out Monica get on your knees and lean over the couch. Neicy you get on top of her in the same position but put your hands on the back of the couch for support." Mike told them.

"Boy you must think we some type of gymnast!" said Neicy.

"All it takes is a little balance." he stated. They assumed the position.

Mike got down on his knees behind Monica. Here it is he had two beautiful pussies and asses in front of him. He thought to himself, "I'm about to put in some work." He put his dick to the entrance of Monica's pussy. As he slid the head in Monica said, "Oh my God!" Mike put his hands on her waist and slowly sunk his dick in to the hilt.

Monica took a deep breath and said, "It's in my stomach!"

Mike said, "Be easy I got you." He slid back slowly pulling out until just the head was in, then he said hold on baby girl and he slammed into her with full force. Monica grunted and shivered as he ferociously pounded her. He took one hand off of her waist and used it to insert two fingers into Neicy's pussy.

Neicy looked back and said, "Bout time!" as she gyrated on his fingers. Mike came up to an almost squatting position and started hitting Monica on a down stroke. Monica put more arch in her back, tooting her ass up. As Mike pounded her, her body started to tremble. He knew she was cumming. After her trembling subsided she collapsed to the floor. Mike said, "One down and one to go!"

Mike then told Neicy, "Come on I got something real creative for you." He laid her on the floor, then lifted both of her legs in the air, crossed them Indian style and pushed them back against her chest. Neicy had never been in a position like that. He lowered himself into her. She was super tight and with only half in she started screaming, "I can't take it, I can't take it!" The more weight Mike put on her legs with his chest the more her ass came up off of the floor and the deeper he went into her. Neicy brought her hands up to put on his chest to relieve some of the pressure that he was applying, but Mike was in a zone banging her back out. He got so deep in her that his balls were slapping her ass crack. He was fucking Neicy into a frenzy.

The pain had started to subside being replaced by pleasure. She let her hands fall away from his chest. Even in an awkward position she was bucking back.

"You a beast! You a beast!" Neicy told him. That set Mike off. He pushed her legs back until her feet were touching her forehead and pounded her relentlessly until he felt that fire rise in his balls. He knew he was about to cum. He let his dick sink all the way into her, then put his hands on her shoulders and started rocking. His body and her body were rocking as he came.

Neicy felt the hot streams shoot into her and started cumming herself. After their orgasms subsided Mike stood up fully soaked with sweat. He looked down at both of them and said, "I guess that saying you heard is true, two is better than one!"

The Head King

Vivian, Marcy and Dena all set up in Vivian's house, talking about how most guys did not give good head. They all had different opinions as to why it was.

"Most of them think they are too good to do it. They only do it when we make them feel obligated by telling them that we ain't sucking their dicks unless they do it. So, they just be going through the motions so that they can get their dicks sucked." Dena said to them.

"They ass be scared that their friends are going to find out. They be thinking that their friends are going to put them on blast if they find out, not even knowing that their friends do it too." Vivian said to them.

"Well I don't have that problem. I think it's about teaching them how to do it. Men are like dogs, you have to teach them tricks. You give them a treat every time they learn a new trick and they will start performing the trick every time you tell them to." Marcy said.

"Bitch! You are crazy. Where you get that bullshit that you are talking from?" Vivian asked her.

"You hoes got me fucked up,"

"I got a jump off that I trained to become a head king."

"I could call Mike right now and he will come over here and suck my pussy while you two sit there and watch."

"That bitch is crazy!" Dena said to Vivian.

"All y'all got to do is put your money where your mouth is."

"Hoe, I'll bet you twenty dollars that it won't happen." Vivian said to her.

"I'll put twenty dollars up too!" Dena jumped in.

"You hoes got a bet." Marcy told them as she flipped open her phone and hit a button. She turned to them, "Yeah, I keep his number on speed dial." Someone answered the phone and Marcy began talking, "Baby I'm over here with these crazy bitches Dena and Vivian. These bitches got me twisted, I want you to come over here and show them why I gave you the name Head King.

"Okay hold on," she turned to Vivian, "What's your address?" She got Vivian's address and repeated it to Mike then hung up the phone.

"He is on his way." Marcy told them as she sat back on the couch.

"This dude has got to be ugly as sin, if he comes over here and sucks this bitch's pussy in front of us." Vivian stated.

"Either that or he's a nerd." Dena replied.

A half an hour went by and there was a knock at the door. Vivian and Dena sat at attention, while Marcy went and opened the door. When Marcy stepped aside to let Mike in, both Vivian and Dena almost fainted. The man that stepped into the house stood at 6' 1" and looked as if he could have been Morris Chestnut's identical twin. Mike smiled at them and they started melting like some M&M's.

"Where do you want to do it at baby?" he asked Marcy.

"We can do it over here." Marcy told him pointing to a reclining chair. She went over by the chair, pulled her skirt up, pulled her panties off, and sat in the chair. Mike took it upon himself and turned the lever on the side of the chair putting her in the reclining position.

He knelt on the floor in front of her like they were the only ones in the room and put both of her legs together. He pushed her legs up and she reached out with her arms and pulled her legs back. She laid there in the chair with her legs pulled back and her pussy sticking out.

Mike reached out with two fingers and stuck them gently inside of her. He moved them around getting them coated with her juices, and he removed them from her pussy and put them in his mouth.

"Ummm!" he moaned as he sucked her juices off of his fingers.

He told Marcy, "Your pussy is so tasty." Right before he lowered his head between her legs. He first put his whole mouth over her pussy and sucked on it. Marcy instantly started to moan. Dena and Vivian sat there looking at the facial expressions that she was making. Next, Mike used two of his fingers from one hand to spread her pussy lips apart, while he took a finger from his other hand and popped her clit, which came to full attention. Mike took his tongue and started licking her clit.

"Shit! Mike that's it, perform for me honey, do that trick." Mike had a gap between his two front teeth and he sucked her clit in between the gap and started flicking his tongue over it. Marcy put her hands on the armrest and lifted her ass up out of the seat. She could not take being still. The pleasure that he was giving her was driving her crazy.

Without Vivian even realizing it, she had stuck her fingers inside of her panties and began playing with herself. Mike dug into his pocket while he continued to eat her pussy and pulled out a little vial and some type of little device. Mike opened the vial and poured some type of liquid out of it into his hand then rubbed his hand on Marcy's pussy. He took the little device that he pulled out of his pocket and slid it onto his fingers. He hit a switch and the device came to life. It started making a vibrating sound and Mike put it on Marcy's pussy.

"Fuck ... fuck ... fuck!" Marcy said out loud. Mike started blowing on her pussy causing the liquid that he had rubbed on it, to start sending a cool sensation all through her body. He rubbed the hand held stimulator on her clit as he blew into her pussy.

"Oh shit Mike!"

"It's cumming baby, oh its cumming!" Marcy said digging her nails into the arms of the chair. She dug them in so far that she put a tear in them. At that moment, she couldn't be concerned with that. The orgasm that was coming out of her body was requiring her full attention. After the orgasm stopped racking her body, Marcy went completely limp in the chair.

Vivian had just reached an orgasm from finger fucking herself, but she did not feel fulfilled. She wanted some of Mike and planned to get some.

"Marcy hoe, I ain't going for that, your ass could be faking. I need to find out for myself if he really is a Head King. He is going to have to eat my shit, for me to know if he's real or not."

"Bitch! That wasn't the bet!" Marcy replied as she lay slumped in the chair.

"Well, I ain't giving my twenty dollars up without finding out for myself."

"I feel what you're saying." Dena jumped in saying.

Marcy knew that they were on some bullshit, but she didn't care. Mike was only a jump off, so she did not care if he put it on them.

"Mike show them bitches what you are working with honey!" Marcy told him.

"It would be my pleasure. Which one of you girls would like to go first?" They both threw their hands in the air at the same time yelling, "Me! Me!"

"Don't worry I have a way to tend to both of you ladies." He had Dena and Vivian stand side by side and pull their clothes down. He had them both bend over, and then he squatted down and began rotating back and forth between them. He began eating them both from the back. He would finger fuck one, while he ate the other's pussy then he would switch.

He sucked on Vivian's pussy as if it was a ripe peach and she came all in his mouth. Dena bent her knees and gyrated her pussy on his face. His tongue was as long as a finger and he stuck it all the way inside of her pussy and wiggled it around, driving her crazy. He made both girls feel so freaky that they started doing something that they had never done in their lives. They turned to each other and began kissing. Mike's tongue had released passion in them that they did not even know they had.

When it was all said and done, they both paid Marcy and voted that Mike was indeed the Head King.

The Contortionist

Rob took a part time job working for a Carnival down at The Gund Arena in Cleveland, Ohio, working as a maintenance man. The Carnival was running for two weeks. While on shift one night Rob received a work order informing him that a fan had stopped working in one of the performer's dressing room.

Rob left his workstation and headed to the dressing room. When he got there he knocked on the door and a voice called out to him, "Come in."

Rob opened the door and stepped into the room. He was shocked by what he seen. On the floor was a girl lying on her back with one of her legs behind her neck. She had on a skimpy bikini and her red pussy hairs were poking out from the sides of it. Rob instantly got a hard on, as he stared at her fat pussy print showing through her suit.

The girl spoke to him breaking his spell, "Hi! My name is Becky, what is yours?" Rob started stuttering, "Uh, uh, my name is Rob and I'm here to fix your fan."

"Sure, I'm glad that you are here, because it has been real hot and stuffy in here. It has been hard for me to practice my routine."

"Where is the fan at?"

"It's sitting right over there on the counter." Rob looked down at her pussy one more time then headed over to the fan.

While he was unscrewing the fan, he looked back over his shoulder and saw that Becky was having a hard time trying to get her other leg behind her neck. He wondered what it was that she actually did in the show.

Becky called out to him, "Hey Rob, could you come give me a hand for a minute?"

Rob set his screwdriver down on the shelf and walked over to Becky, "What can I help you with?"

"Could you pull my leg back a little bit for me, so that I can get a good hold of it?"

"You mean bend your leg back? That looks dangerous and I don't want to hurt you."

"Don't worry you can't hurt me, I'm a contortionist."

"What is that?"

"That means that I can bend my body parts all type of ways. It is like my joints are made of elastic. That is what I do in my show. Push my leg back and I will show you." Rob grabbed her leg and tried to carefully push it back. All of a sudden, he heard a loud pop and her leg became loose in his hand. Her leg popped out of its joints, but he seen no sign of pain on Becky's face.

She took her hands and pulled her leg the rest of the way back and put it behind her neck. With both of her legs behind her head, Becky's pussy was poking out. Rob looked at her face and took in that she was kind of homely looking. She had freckles on her face and her hair was in pig tails.

He thought to himself, "She may look homely, but her pussy looks good as hell. Becky broke him out of his trance for the second time, when she told him, "Thanks, I have to get loose for the show."

Rob told her, "You're welcome." then went back over to the fan.

Rob had taken the fan apart, found the problem and fixed it. He was putting the screws back in, when Becky called out to him, "Are you almost finished?" Rob turned around and found her in a different position. She was off of the floor and walking around on her hands, with her legs still behind her head. First thing that Rob thought to himself when he seen her in that position was, "I would sure love to fuck her like that." He told her, "Yeah, all I have to do is put the screws in."

"Have you ever seen my show?" she asked him.

"Unfortunately not, I am on the clock."

"I like you, you're kind of cute."

"What if I promise to give you a private show, would you give me a ride to my hotel room after the show?" Rob did not even have to debate about what she asked.

He blurted out, "Hell yeah, I will do it!"

"Okay, my last show should end at ten o'clock, meet me back here then?"

"Bet!" Rob told her, then grabbed his tools and left her dressing room.

He whistled all the way back to his workstation. He was looking forward to that night. Becky left her room headed to the stage to perform. She was looking forward to that night as well.

Becky knew that she was homely looking. Coming up she never got much attention from the boys. Once she learned that she had a special talent she tried to use it to attract boys. She found that her gift did not always work.

Sometimes showing them her talent would scare the boys off. They would laugh at her and call her a freak. To feel some type of acceptance, Becky decided to join a traveling circus. She found that there were many men that watched the show and wanted to show her attention afterwards. Rob seemed nice and he did not look at her in a weird way like a lot of others did. He looked at her in a sexual way and that excited Becky.

Becky performed her two shows then headed back to her dressing room. When she entered her room, she was surprised to see Rob inside waiting on her.

"How long have you been here?" she asked him. Rob looked at his watch and responded, "About forty five minutes."

"Wow! Just let me grab my things and we can go."

Becky gathered her things and they left. She directed him to a hotel on the west side of town. They arrived to her hotel room. Once inside Becky told him she was going to give him the, "Version."

She went into her bag and pulled out a few items, and then she told him to take a seat in the chair that sat directly across from the bed. Rob went over to the chair and sat down. Becky stripped down to her bikini and started performing. First she did regular things, like hand stands and full splits, then she did things like put her hands together and put them behind her back. Just when things were starting to get boring to Rob, Becky grabbed two items that sparked his interest and laid them onto the bed.

She had a plastic bag full of ping pong balls and a large dildo. She took off her bottoms revealing a bush of red hair. This caused Rob to sit up in his seat. She climbed onto the bed and grabbed the bag of ping pong balls, then went to lie back on the bed. She raised her head up and looked at Rob.

"I hope you can catch." she told him then put her head back down. She took a ball out of the bag. She spread her legs out and then inserted the ping pong ball inside of her pussy.

"Are you ready?" she asked Rob. Before he could answer the ping pong came flying out of her at him. He quickly put his hands up and caught it, and Becky started laughing as she inserted three more balls inside of her pussy.

"Here they come!" she said before shooting the three balls at him. They all shot out back to back. Rob could not believe what he was seeing, but he did catch all of the balls.

Becky stacked two pillows up behind her, then grabbed the dildo and told him, "That's not all that can shoot out of my pussy, watch this." She then took the dildo and inserted it in her pussy. She started fucking herself with the dildo. Rob's dick was so swollen that it hurt.

He was ready to say fuck the show and just ask her for some pussy. He had no doubt in his mind that he was fucking that night. It was all a matter of when she was ready for it. He moved up to the edge of his seat, when she got to talking dirty.

"I love fucking myself. I know how to make my pussy feel good. If you come closer, you will see how much cream my pussy has put all over this dildo."

"Come over here and see."

Rob got up off from the chair and went over to the bed. He got onto the bed to lie sideways and looked closely at the dildo going in and out of her pussy. He grabbed his dick and squeezed it, wishing that he had it inside of her pussy. Becky started breathing hard and told him, "Get closer so you can see it come out, when I come." Rob put his face just inches away from her pussy as she began fucking herself hard with the dildo.

"It is on the way, don't miss the show!" she said to Rob then began skeeting. A glob of cum hit Rob on his nose and he jumped back and said, "Hey! What the fuck!" He stood up off of the bed and continued watching as cum shot out of her pussy.

"I told you that other things shot out!" Becky said giggling.

"We are going to see what's funny!" Rob said to her as he began taking off his clothes.

When he was naked standing before Becky, she said, "That looks like it is about to break. I don't think your dick is flexible like me."

"Well, we are about to find out because I'm about to ram it in you."

"What position do you want first?"

"The one that you were in earlier."

"You mean this one?" she asked him then began putting her legs behind her head. When she got both legs behind her head her pussy sat out and her lips were open. Rob jumped on the bed and put his dick into her. He did not even start off slow he went right to pounding her. Her pelvis bone was hurting him, so he picked her up off of the bed and began fucking himself with her. Her legs were behind her neck as he held her from the side and moved her up and down on his dick. It was almost as if he was fucking a paraplegic.

"That a boy, fuck this pussy, I never been fucked this way!" she told him. Rob looked at her and said, "What other positions do you got?"

"Put me down and I will show you." Rob put Becky down and she unfolded herself. She stayed on her back and pushed herself up until she was bent all the way over backwards with her hands and feet on the floor.

"Try this," she said to Rob. It was an awkward position to fuck someone in and Rob had to figure out how to do it. He did a move that he had learned from playing twister. He put one leg inside of her leg, then bent over her sideways and put his dick into her. Becky lowered her ass then raised it up to fuck him. He had to keep both of his hands on the floor in order to keep his balance. He fucked her like that for a few minutes then got another idea. He went around in front of her and squatted down in front of her face. He put his dick to her mouth and she sucked it in. In the position that she was in, she could not use nothing but her neck. She used it to give him the best head action that he had in a long time.

They finished the night out with her standing straight up then pulling her left leg up backwards holding it in the air like a figure skater, while Rob put his hands on her shoulder and fucked her standing up. Rob busted many nuts that night and left Becky's hotel room thinking, "Now I know what it means to be bent out of shape."

Size Don't Matter

Richard had a date planned with Veronica and was getting ready. His boy Corey was sitting up in his living room playing the PlayStation. When Richard came downstairs, Corey said to him, "Damn playboy you been going out with old girl for about a month now. When are you going to hook me up with one of her friends?"

"I ain't got time to play no matchmaker."

"I ain't asking you to play matchmaker. I'm just saying look out for your boy, see if she has a friend."

"She only has one friend, but you wouldn't like her."

"Man, you don't know my taste! You don't know what I like."

"I know you won't like her friend."

"Why don't you let me be the judge of that?"

"Okay, you want to meet her friend? You got that, I'm about to call Veronica right now, but I swear I don't want to hear your mouth after you meet her friend."

"Just make the call." Richard called Veronica and told her to call her friend Mildred and have her to come over because he had somebody that wanted to meet her. He hung up and turned to Corey, "Come on let's go." They got into Richard's truck and headed over to Veronica's house. Corey asked him what Veronica's friend name was, "It's Mildred," he told him.

Corey was hyped, because as fine and stuck up as Veronica was, he knew that she did not have any ugly friends. He figured that Richard just did not want to put him on, because he considered Corey as a player and did not want Veronica to think the same thing about him.

They pulled up in Veronica's driveway. They got out of the truck and went up to the door. Richard knocked on the door and Veronica opened it. They stepped in and she closed the door behind them. She offered them a seat and as soon as Corey sat down he asked, "So where is Mildred at?"

"She will be down in a minute." Veronica told him.

She asked Richard, "So are we still going out or are we going to stay in?"

"We are going to go out for a couple of drinks."

"That's cool," she told him then she called upstairs to Mildred, "Girl come on we are about to go."

In what sounded like a baby's voice Corey heard someone say, "Here I come." He turned towards the stairs and could not believe his eyes, when what seemed to be a miniature woman appeared at the top of the steps.

Corey watched on in amazement as the little figure had to grab onto the banister for support as her little bowed legs carried her down the stairs. When she got to the bottom of the steps, Corey took in the fact that she couldn't have been any more than three and a half feet tall.

"Hell no!" he said then jumped up.

"Richard, let me holla at you outside for a minute." Richard frowned, then reluctantly got up and headed to the door with Corey following behind him. He opened the door and they stepped out onto the porch and Richard closed the door behind him.

Inside Mildred already knew what the problem was.

"You didn't tell him I was a midget did you?" she asked Veronica.

"I never talked to him."

"Richard called me and told me to call you."

"Girl don't even trip, if he gets to acting funny fuck him!" Mildred was happy when Veronica called and told her that she had somebody that wanted to meet her. People seldom wanted to meet her once they found out that she was a midget. And the ones that did not know that she was a midget before they met her face to face always seemed to find an excuse not to kick it with her once they seen her size.

Out on the porch Richard and Corey were going back and forth.

"Man you could of told me that she was a midget!"

"Forget all that, I tried to tell you that you wouldn't like her. I know you think that you are God's gift to women and that you can't mess around with a girl who you think might cramp your style. You pressed me, even after I told you that you wouldn't like her."

"I thought that she would at least be a regular sized girl."

"You acted like you did not care if she was a Martian. I did what you asked me to and we are here now, so you are going out with her and you are going to treat her right."

"Yeah whatever!" Corey told Richard as he opened the door and stepped back into the house.

"Are you two ready?" Richard asked them.

"Yeah, we are ready." Veronica responded. They all headed outside to Richard's truck, and Corey walked around to the driver's side and opened the back door to get in.

"Are you going to leave her in the driveway?" Richard yelled to Corey. Corey realized that Mildred was too small to even reach the door handle on the truck. He ran back around to the other side.

"I'm sorry!" he said to Mildred then opened the door for her. He knew that she couldn't climb up in the truck by herself and that she needed help.

"You don't mind if I help you do you?" he asked her nervously.

"Pick me up, I ain't going to break." Corey put his hands on her waist, picked her up and put her into the truck. He noticed that she was real heavy for her size. Once he closed her door he went around and climbed into the truck.

Richard drove to a bar so that they could have drinks. When they got there, Corey got out and went around and helped Mildred out of the truck. When he put her on the ground he followed behind her as they headed into the bar. He noticed how her body was shaped like a full sized woman even though she was miniature. He looked at her small waist and fat ass. To be so small she had an ass that a stripper would love.

When they got into the bar, Corey was about to help Mildred to get up on a stool, when she told him, "I got it." She took her little hands and pulled herself up onto the bar stool. Corey took a seat next to her and asked her what she wanted to drink. She told him that she wanted a shot of Grey Goose. He ordered both of them drinks.

Richard and Veronica went onto the little dance floor to dance, while Corey and Mildred sat drinking shots. After about three shots, Corey started taking in how big her titties were and how pretty she looked. He thought to himself, "If she was full size she would be bad." Mildred was buzzing and saw how he was looking at her and knew what he was thinking.

"I may be small, but I can do anything that a girl twice my size can."

"What are you talking about?"

"I see how you are looking at me. You wish I was regular size, so you could fuck the shit out of me, but for your information, I will fuck you until you beg me to stop." Corey laughed and said, "Yeah right, I will tear your little ass up."

"My pussy is probably too big for your dick anyway."

"You talk a lot of shit to be as small as you are. You keep talking that big shit and I'm going to have to put it on your little ass."

"Get Richard's keys." she said to him.

"Are you serious?"

"What you scared? Go get his keys." Corey went out onto the dance floor and asked Richard for the keys to his truck.

"What you want my keys for, you ain't about to leave?"

"No man, Mildred wants to go out to the truck." Richard started smiling, "Oh, okay handle your business fam!"

He gave his keys to Corey and winked at him. Corey went back over to Mildred.

"Let's go, it's time to see what your little ass is working with."

He helped her down off of the stool and they headed out to the truck. Corey unlocked the front door opened it, and then he unlocked the backdoor. He opened the backdoor and folded the backseat down, making the whole back area of the floor flat. He then picked Mildred up and put her inside climbing in behind her. Before he even had the door closed Mildred was coming out of her clothes. Corey closed the door and watched her undress. She didn't just take her clothes off, she did a seductive striptease. Corey decided to help her out. He climbed into the front seat, put the key in the ignition and turned the CD on.

Mildred quickly caught the beat and started dancing to it. When she began taking off her clothes things started to change for Corey. All that about her being small went out the door. When her titties became freed, he saw that they were at least a size 32D. They set up high and looked so delicious to him. Her nipples were big as dimes. He couldn't control his self and reached out and grabbed one. He squeezed it and it felt so good in his hand.

Mildred just kept dancing and removing her clothing. She had to back away from him so that she could take off her pants. When she took them off she had ass everywhere. Corey did not even know that they made thongs that small. Mildred turned towards him so that he could see both of her perfectly shaped ass cheeks. They were the color of a Hershey's chocolate bar and looked just as rich as one.

Corey felt his dick swell to a size that it had never reached before. He could not understand how someone so small could have a body like Mildred's. It was crazy because Mildred was standing straight up in the truck and still had room to raise her hands. She slid her thong off and laid down on her back with her legs in the air. Mildred began making them shake like a stripper does.

Corey watched as from her feet down to her ass cheeks shook, but what sent him over the top was when she went to spread her legs open. He was amazed at how fat her pussy lips were. They were some of the fattest lips that he had ever saw, covered by a thick hairy bush. He could no longer keep his dick inside of his pants.

"Enough of this bullshit!" he said to himself as he started taking his clothes off. Mildred rose up on her little arms and watched him strip. She started licking her lips when she saw him taking off his pants. Corey was so tall that he had to sit down to pull his pants and drawers off. After he got them off he got up on his knees and Mildred crawled over to him.

"You big, but you still can't hang. I'm going to put this head game on you first." she told him as she bent down to give him head without using her hands. She put her hands behind her back and just gave him neck action. Both of her jaws puffed out as she was sucking him off. Corey put his hands under her and started playing with her titties. He massaged them and rubbed her nipples in between his fingers. That only aroused Mildred more and   she gave him some of the best head that he had ever had in his life.

"Your head is fire Mildred. Damn you can suck a dick." Mildred backed up off of his dick.

"Wait 'til you get in this pussy. It's going to suck you in."

"You want to get on top so I don't hurt you?" he asked her.

"Shit, you the one that's going to be hurting, lay down." she told him. Corey laid flat on his back and Mildred straddled him.

She put both of her little feet on the side of him and lowered herself onto his dick. Corey raised his head to watch his dick go in her.

He knew he was at least nine inches and had made many girls cry. He just knew that Mildred's little ass wasn't going to be able to take him all the way in. Her little pudgy hands couldn't even fit around his dick as she used them to guide his dick to her entrance. She lowered herself onto him and he watched unbelievably as she sank all the way down on his dick until he could feel her pussy hairs on his pelvis.

Her pussy was so hot and wet and as soon as she started moving back and forth on his dick he could hear the sloshing sounds that her pussy was making. She was facing him, looking at the fuck faces that he was making as she rode him.

"You like that don't you, feels good don't it? This little bitch got some bomb pussy doesn't she? Don't be scared to tell me, I know it's good. This dick is good too. It's like riding a roller coaster." Mildred bent down and started sucking on Corey's chest. She nibbled on his nipples and licked around them. She had Corey lying there whimpering.

"This is where I put it on you." she told him and then she put her feet up, put her hands on the floor and spun herself around on his dick until she was facing away from him. Corey could not believe that she had just spun around on his dick like a person would do on a sit and spin.

He knew from that day on that he was not going to judge anything just off of looks. Mildred put her little feet on top of his thighs and put her hands on his waist and started riding him reversed cowgirl style. She started slamming her body down onto him. Her ass cheeks shook every time she slammed them down on him.

Corey was breathing hard and moaning like he was the one that was getting fucked and Mildred wasn't making it any better.

"Take it, don't bitch up, Mildred works this pussy, y'all think Mildred be playing. Watch how these pussy muscles pull that nut out of you." Mildred started doing something that Corey had never witnessed before. She started constricting her pussy muscles. Mildred made her pussy tighten up on his dick then loosen up.

"You little fucker, here it comes, take it then." Mildred moved her feet off of his thighs and flopped down onto him and sat there.

"Blast off then mother fucker." she said to him.

Corey came so hard that his eyes started to water. He was still cumming, when they heard a tap on the window. He turned his head to the window and Richard and Veronica seen the ugly look that he had on his face. They both started laughing and turned their backs so that they could get themselves together.

Mildred put all of her clothes back on, but Corey laid on the floor ass naked. Richard turned back and seen that he still did not have his clothes on. He yelled through the window, "Put your clothes on!"

Corey yelled back, "I can't, I think I'm paralyzed." Richard shook his head, then him and Veronica climbed into the front seat and he took off. Mildred stood in between the driver and passenger's seat smiling.

Richard looked into the rearview mirror and said, "What happened man?" Corey responded, "Big things come in small packages."

Mildred turned and said, "Are you ready for round two?" she got ready to dive on Corey. Corey saw her coming through the air and screamed, "Nooooooo!"

Pussy Pounders

Marie got off of work one Friday evening and while walking to her car, she pulled out a flyer that she had been given earlier in the week by one of her co-workers. She unfolded the flyer and read it. The heading said, "Come to an all-male review at the Gentlemen Persuasion. See the Pussy Pounders performs two shows." Also on the flyer, was a picture of a black guy that was built like a God. The only thing that he had on was a G-string, which let the print of his package be seen.

Marie's mouth started to water as she looked at the fine black God on the flyer. She did not have a man because of her long work hours and her ambition to get ahead in life. She did have a couple sex partners that she would call whenever she wanted a booty call, but she was getting fed up with them. Neither George nor Carl could hit the pussy right for some reason. She thought to herself, "It's going to take both of them together to fulfill my needs. I want a man that gives it to me like I need it, somebody like him on this flyer."

Marie could not see herself going into a strip club by herself, so when she got in her car, she flipped open her phone and called her friend Rita.

Rita had been her friend since they were teenagers. She knew that Rita had a man, but she also knew that he wasn't shit. Marie felt that James did not appreciate Rita and that all he did was keep her stressed out. She knew that Rita was probably sitting at home waiting on James to come in from the streets. She wanted her friend to join her out for a night of fun.

Rita answered her phone, "Hello?"

"What are you doing girl?"

"Just sitting here watching TV, why?"

"I want you to go out with me tonight?"

"Go out where?"

"To the GP,"

"The GP, ain't that a strip club?"

"Yeah, they are having a male review tonight, the Pussy Pounders are performing."

"Girl you are trying to get me killed. If James found out that I went to a strip club, he would kill me!"

"You always worried about James sorry ass. Where is his ass at right now?"

"I don't know,"

"Exactly, that's my point!

Who's to say that he ain't up in a strip club right now?

If he can go out, then so can you!"

"Yeah, but a strip club?"

"Rita, I'm not asking you to fuck nobody. I just want you to go out with me and have some fun. Can you do that for me?"

"Okay girl I'll go, come and get me."

"That's my girl, I'm going home to take a shower and get dressed, and then I will be on my way." Marie closed her phone, started her car and headed home. When she got home, she took a shower and changed clothes. She wanted to feel sexy, so she put on a sheer black blouse, a short black mini skirt and some black patent leather pumps.

She decided that she wasn't going to wear any underwear. If something happened, she wanted the person to have easy access. She sprayed perfume on her neck, chest and her pussy. Once she was finished she grabbed her car keys and headed out the door. She got into her car and headed over to Rita's.

She parked in Rita's driveway, got out and went to her door. She rang the bell and Rita opened the door. She looked at Marie's outfit and put her hand up to her mouth.

"Bitch what?" Marie asked her.

"You look like you are trying to get fucked tonight?"

"I done well then, because that's the look that I was trying to get. Get your shit and let's go." Rita grabbed her purse and they left.

When they pulled up to the GP, they could not believe how crowded the streets were. Both sides of the streets had their parking spaces filled, and the little parking lot next to the GP was filled to capacity. Marie had to park two blocks away and they had to walk back to the club.

There was a long line outside of the club and it took them over thirty minutes to get inside. When they got inside they were shoulder to shoulder with people as they tried to make their way up to the bar.

When they got to the bar it was the same thing a long line. They waited until their turn came and ordered their drinks.

Marie knew that she was going to want more than one drink and she wasn't for having to stand in no long line again. She ordered herself two doubles of Hennessy straight with no chaser.

She got her drinks and went looking for a table to sit at with Rita following behind her. When she entered the side of the bar where the strippers were doing their thing, the music was blasting. Nelly's song, *Shake your tail feather*, was playing and Marie started shaking her ass as she walked. The place was packed with women and some had to stand against the walls because they had no seats. The only men that were in the place were the ones that were working the room.

The male strippers were moving throughout the room giving out lap dances, shaking their asses and dicks in the faces of the inviting woman. Most of them had on too small G-strings that left little to the imagination. Some of them were walking around with their balls hanging out. Some of them had their dicks popping free as they shook them in front of the ladies faces. None of the women had a problem and they all loved what was going on.

The DJ announced that the show was about to begin and that the Pussy Pounders were about to take the stage. Marie was getting upset, because she could not find a place to sit. She could not even get a spot up close to the stage to see the action. She and Rita had to stand on their toes in the middle of the isle to see them perform.

The Pussy Pounders had the ladies up front going crazy from the dancing and the tricks that they were doing. They even pulled some women up onto the stage with them and performed with them. Marie was mad that she couldn't see the show. All she could do was see them from their chest up, when they were standing up.

After they finished their show, the Pussy Pounders jumped off of the stage and started mingling in the audience.

"Come on!" Marie said to Rita as she went to find her a place on the wall to stand. She wanted to be able to watch the floor, because she knew that they were going to perform another show. She wanted to watch for someone getting out of their seat so that she could get it.

After about ten minutes she saw a group of girls get up from a table that was close to the stage. She grabbed Rita's hand and took off headed for the seats. They got to them and they sat down. Rita was still upset because she had spilled all of her second drink pushing through the crowd.

When the DJ announced that the second show would be starting in ten minutes, the four girls that had been sitting at the table popped back up, "Excuse us, but you two are sitting in our seats!" one of them said.

"Well, we did not see anybody sitting here, when we sat down." Marie said to the girl.

"That's because we took a restroom break." one of the other girls jumped in saying.

"Come on, let's go!" Rita said to Marie, not wanting any trouble with the four girls.

"Fuck that! I ain't missing this show!" Marie responded.

"You bitches are going to have to watch it from somewhere else." One of the girls told them.

"Who are you calling a bitch?" Marie said jumping up out of her seat. The Pussy Pounders were making their way back to the stage and witnessed the confrontation. They stood in front of the stage and watched the bouncers clear up the problem. The four girls explained the situation to the bouncers and Marie was told by the bouncers that she and Rita would have to find someplace else to watch the show.

Marie and one of the Pussy Pounders locked eyes and looked each other up and down before she walked off. Since she couldn't see the show, she decided to go and order another drink.

Since the show was going on, there wasn't a line at the bar. Marie ordered her and Rita another drink, and headed back to the other side. Marie had made up her mind that she was going to at least get a lap dance before she left, even if she had to get it while she was standing up. Her and Rita found a place against the wall and sipped their drinks.

After the show the Pussy Pounders jumped off stage again and started mingling with the audience. They made their way over to where Marie and Rita were standing, and the one that had locked eyes with Marie earlier seen her and approached her.

He noticed that she still had an evil look on her face. He asked her, "What was that all about earlier, with you and those other girls?" Marie just looked at him for a minute. She was buzzing and ready to act a fool, because she had to park two blocks away then paid a ten dollar admittance fee and didn't get to see shit. Now here he was standing in front of her like he was concerned. She wanted to see how concerned he really was.

"I had to park two blocks away and walk down here, I paid ten dollars to get in, and I couldn't find a seat or get close enough to see the first show. I saw those girls leave so I sat down hoping to be able to see the second show. Those hoes tripped, so I missed that one too."

"You went through all that and missed both shows. How about this, let the Pussy Pounders make it up to you and your friend?"

"And how are you going to do that?"

"You know that they have a V.I.P room. I'm going to pay for the admittance out of my own pocket and I and my partner are going to give you two a private show." Marie started to cheer up.

"You would do that?"

"For someone as beautiful as you, I would try to conquer the world." Marie couldn't do nothing but blush. He said something to his partner, then grabbed Marie's hand and led her away. His partner grabbed Rita's hand and followed him. He led her to a red curtain that he pulled aside. They all entered into a hallway, and he led them to a door and tapped on it. A big burly guy opened the door and the Pussy Ponder that held Marie's hand said something into his ear. He stepped aside and let them in. They went in and entered another room and closed the door. They were in a room that had a couch, a love seat, a bar and a stereo system.

The Pounder let go of Marie's hand, "Have a seat." he told her. She took a seat on the couch and Rita took a seat on the love seat. He went over, turned on the stereo, then walked back over in front of Marie and started dancing. Marie sat there sipping her drink and looking at him at the same time. He looked like a sex God to her. He stood well over six feet and he had muscles bulging from everywhere.

There was definition in his chest, arms and thighs. He was so black that you would think he had just come over from Africa, fresh off the boat. Marie's pussy started getting wet when she looked at his dick. It looked like he had two pair of socks stuffed into his G-string.

She did not know what made her do it but she reached out and grabbed his dick. He didn't even trip he came closer to her and put his foot up on the couch next to her. Marie continued to massage his dick, while they looked each other in the eyes. She put her other hand on it and started massaging his dick and balls. She closed her eyes and started imagining how it would feel to have his dick inside of her. From the way his dick felt balled up in the G-string, she thought that it was bigger than her two fuck partner's dicks put together.

Rita sat on the other couch not believing her eyes. The other guy was dancing in front of her, but she was watching Marie. She wanted to say something but she seen that Marie was in a zone. She was hoping that the guy that was dancing for her did not get the same impression. She had no intention of doing anything sexual. She turned her head away, when she seen Marie pull the guy's dick out of his G-string. It uncoiled like a snake and was so long that it bent down in the front.

Marie took both of her hands and rubbed it. She held it while it expanded to its full length in her hands. The Pussy Pounder reached his hand up under her skirt and found that she did not have any panties on. He slipped two fingers inside of her and started fucking her with them.

Marie lowered her mouth onto his dick. She kept both of her hands on it as she sucked his dick, being as she could not get more than half into her mouth. The Pussy Pounder told her, "Your head game is invaluable, but I must show you why they call me the Pussy Pounder." He pulled her up then picked her up with one arm. She was amazed at how strong he was, he held her up completely in the air with one arm and used his hand on his other arm to guide his dick into her. Once he got his dick in, he put his hands up under her shoulders and started moving her up and down on his dick. Marie held her legs out wide like she was a gymnastics performer. Rita could not keep herself from looking at what Marie was doing. She was trying to ignore the guy that was standing in front of her with his dick in her face, but watching Marie getting fucked was turning her on. She did not even realize that her skirt was up until she felt something cool and wet on her pussy. She looked down and the Pussy Pounder was in between her legs sucking her pussy through her panties. She wanted to stop him, but the feeling was just too good.

She did away with the block that she tried to keep up and just let herself go. The Pussy Pounder pulled her panties to the side and started feeding himself her pussy.

"Damn it feels so good!" Rita said to herself. She did not care anymore that he wasn't James. She didn't care that she was in a room with other people.

"Let me see it?" she asked him. He got up and stepped out of his G-string, "Jesus, you are a heaven send, please put it in me?"

"My pleasure!" he told her as he spread her legs. She laid back on the back of the loveseat. With his feet still on the floor he leaned over her and put his dick inside of her. She looked in lust as his dick went in and out of her. It looked like the length of a ruler was inside of her and half of that length was still outside of her.

She creamed on his dick just from watching his dick go in and out of her.

"Ummm!" she moaned as she came.

The Pussy Party

Michelle was having a sex toy party. She had invited her friends over to try and sell them some sex toys that she had bought wholesale. She invited four of her friends over to have refreshments and look at the toys.

By eight o'clock all of her friends had arrived. Kayla, Rosie, Danielle and Panzie, were all mingling in Michelle's living room. Michelle had toys sitting on table stands next to the drinks and refreshments. The girls would pick them up and look at them. After the girls had a couple of drinks, Michelle had them all take a seat so that she could tell them about the toys, how they worked and how much they cost.

Buzzing, the girls were laughing and cracking jokes as she explained how the toys she showed them worked. She put one item on her hand and hit a switch. The little device came to life making a buzzing sound.

"This is a handheld pussy stimulator." she explained to them as she demonstrated for them by placing it on the back of her hand.

"That thing is small." Kayla said.

"Yeah, it's compact so you can take it anywhere with you." Michelle told her.

Michelle put the stimulator down and picked up a huge, black dildo.

"This here is made out of rubber and is very flexible."

"How long is it?" Rosa asked.

"It's nine and a half inches, so there shouldn't be any problem finding your g-spot."

"I know that's right!" Panzi jumped in saying. Next, Michelle showed them a two headed dildo.

"What the hell is a girl supposed to do with that?" Kayla asked her.

"It is flexible, so you can use it on yourself for double penetration or you could use it with someone else."

"Well, before I spend my money, I want to see a demonstration to see if those things really work." Rosa said. The room fell silent at her suggestion. No one in the room was a lesbian or at least let it be known that they were one.

"Shit, y'all acting like I said something crazy. I want to see if those things really work before I spend my hard earn money. If I got to be the one to volunteer, so be it."

"Y'all are not going to care if I show this bitch, are you?"

"If she wants you playing in her shit go ahead." Danielle told Michelle.

"This about to be some Jerry Springer shit!" Panzi said.

All the girls had drunk several drinks and were buzzing.

"Okay I'm going to get a blanket and bring it out here." Michelle said then went up to her room. She came back downstairs with a blanket and made a pallet on the floor.

"Take your pants and panties off." she said to Rosa. Rosa walked over to the pallet, took off her shoes, and pulled her pants and panties off. She wasn't embarrassed at all. The other girls just sat there waiting for the show.

Michelle grabbed a hand full of toys then walked over to the pallet. She knelt down and put all of the toys onto the pallet.

"Which one do you want to try first?" she asked Rosa.

"It's your demonstration, whatever you choose." Michelle put the hand held stimulator onto her hand and turned it on. Rosa leaned back on her elbows and opened her legs. Michelle used one of her hands to separate Rosa's pussy lips then she used the other hand to put the stimulator on her clit. As she rubbed the stimulator on her clit, she got the urge to stick two of her fingers inside of Rosa. Rosa sighed, when the two fingers slid inside of her. The combination of the stimulator and the fingers had her pussy on fire, and she began to gyrate her hips.

"That shit feels good. Let me see what that Dildo feels like." Michelle reached over and grabbed the dildo. She kept the stimulator on her clit as she sunk the dildo inside of her pussy. She sunk the dildo all the way in.

"Good God Yes!" Michelle started fucking her with the dildo, and Rosa brought her knees up and pulled her legs back. The other girls started having different feelings as to what was going on.

Danielle turned away thinking that it went from a demonstration to something that was sexual. Kayla got turned on, and got up off of the couch and walked over to the pallet. She got down on the pallet and said, "Let me do it." Michelle turned the dildo over to her and she started moving it all around in Rosa's pussy.

"Does it feel good?" she asked her.

"Hell yeah!" Rosa responded.

"I want to try it, do me." she said to Michelle then started taking off her clothes.

Kayla took off her pants and panties and got onto the floor in the doggy style position.

"Do me from the back."

"Let me do her!" Rosa told Michelle. Rosa got up on her knees, on the side of Kayla and slid the dildo into her pussy.

"Hold her cheeks open, so I can see it going in." Rosa told Michelle. Michelle straddled Kayla's back, bent over and used her hands to spread her ass cheeks. Her and Rosa watched Kayla's pussy suck the dildo in every time she pulled it out.

"She got some fat pussy lips!" Rosa said out loud. Panzi got up and joined them on the floor. She wanted to see the action close up. She had never been up close on another woman's pussy, and seeing how Kayla's pussy was clinging to the dildo was turning her own.

"I use to watch porno tapes and always wondered what a woman's pussy tasted like, when I would see them eating each other. I guess this is the perfect time." Rosa said then pulled the dildo out of Kayla's pussy and put her mouth down there.

She started sucking Kayla's pussy from the back. It just came natural to her and she knew that she was doing it right when Kayla told her, "Do that shit then bitch, suck this pussy." Michelle reached onto the floor, grabbed a bottle of oil and opened it. She put some of the oil in her hand, picked up the dildo then rubbed the oil on it. After she had it oiled up she put it to Kayla's asshole. She pushed and the head popped in, "Good graces!" Kayla said, when she started fucking her in the ass   with the dildo.

Rosa was squatting eating Kayla's pussy when Panzie picked up the stimulator and put it to her pussy. Michelle was fucking Kayla in the ass with the dildo, Rosa was sucking Kayla's pussy from the back and Panzie was using the stimulator on Rosa's pussy. The only one that was left out was Danielle.

Michelle called over to her, "Bitch! You might as well stop acting funny and join the pussy party." Danielle got up and went over to the pallet.

"I will use something on somebody, but I ain't on that other stuff" she said.

Michelle got up and said, "Try this," She grabbed the two headed dildo. She put it into Kayla's pussy, while she still had the other dildo in her ass. Rosa got on her knees facing away from Kayla and backed up on the dildo. Panzie guided it into her pussy. Kayla and Rosa both fucked the dildo. Panzie said fuck being left out. She quickly took off her clothes and put her pussy in Rosa's face and Rosa eagerly started lapping it. Michelle got undressed laid down and put the pussy stimulator on her pussy. Danielle was like enough is enough, and dropped down beside Michelle. She took the stimulator from her and started rubbing her clit with it.

Michelle was breathing hard and gyrating her hips. She was trying to fuck the stimulator.

"Damn Danielle, I'm cumming already. Do it just like that." Danielle kept her rhythm and the next thing she knew, Michelle's pussy was pumping cum out onto her hand. Her pussy pumped a whole lot of cum out. She knew that Michelle had got a good nut. She said to herself, "Fuck it," She stood up and pulled her clothes off so that she could join the pussy party.

Happy Birthday

Cara got frustrated and pulled the vibrator out of her pussy, and threw it onto the floor. She then fell back onto her pillow brooding. She had been miserable for the last two years ever since Mike had broken up with her. Even after two years, Cara still couldn't figure out what she had done wrong. Mike had kept begging her to have a threesome. She put him off for the longest, but he wouldn't let it go, so she finally gave in.

They had a threesome with one of Mike's friends and everything was okay at first. When Cara was uncomfortable and nervous, Mike was fine, but when she started to enjoy herself Mike got upset.

Cara had reached multiple orgasms while having the threesome and afterwards, Mike became infuriated. He called her sluts and whores and started accusing her of liking his friend Richard. Two weeks after the threesome, Mike told Cara that he did not want to be involved with her anymore.

Cara fell into a deep depression. She has always been a little overweight. Cara weighed 175 pounds, but when the depression kicked in she ballooned to almost 300 pounds. This was because she had found solace in food.

Cara had gotten so big that she seldom had any energy to get out of bed. Before Mike left, Cara was having sex three to four times a day. Since he had left, her sex life had become nonexistent. She had resorted to using a vibrator eighteen months ago, but it was no longer satisfying her and that was why she had thrown it to the floor. She yearned for physical contact. She wanted to be touched and to be able to touch someone else.

The next day was going to be her birthday and she knew that she wouldn't be doing anything, but sitting up in the house. She figured that her sister Carry would probably come over to try and cheer her up. Her sister was also her friend. She was really the only friend that she had. Carry did her best to try and help her get over Mike and to get her life back on track.

Cara was still lying in bed naked from the waist down, when her phone rang. She reached down on the side of her, where she kept her phone and picked it up. She answered it, "Hello Carry!" she said into the phone, knowing that it could only be her sister calling.

"How are you doing sis?"

"I'm okay, I guess."

"I was calling to see what it is that you wanted to do tomorrow for your birthday?"

"I wish that I could get laid." Carry knew that her sister was serious about what she had said. She knew that she hasn't had sex in two years and wished that she could help her. She did not understand how her sister could let a man cause her to destroy her life. Her health was in danger all because of a man. It had been two years and she wasn't giving up on trying to get her sister back to the way she used to be. She was intending on trying to cheer her up for her birthday.

"Well, I'm coming over tomorrow with some cake and ice cream and if you feel like going out, then maybe we could go boy hunting." Cara laughed, because she knew that her sister was only trying to cheer her up.

"Okay, that's fine she responded."

"I will see you tomorrow." her sister told her then hung up.

Carry sat there trying to figure out what she could do to cheer her sister up. An idea came to her head.

"I will get some strippers to dance for her." she went to her computer and went online looking for dancers for hire. She was surfing the web when she came across a site called the Mandingo Click. She clicked onto the site and seen the pictures of three men all of which were black. She read their profiles and how much they charged for their performances. She looked and seen that their price was reasonable, so she wrote their number down and gave them a call.

Their representative answered the phone and Carry explained what she was looking for to him. They discussed the time, the price and the place. Carry gave him the address and he assured her that the Mandingo Click would be there on time.

Carry hung up the phone happy. She knew that the Mandingo Click would make her sister's day. She thought that she might be able to offer one of them some extra money to have sex with Cara.

ᛐ

The next day at about 8pm, Carry arrived over to Cara's house. She used the key that her sister had given her to let herself in. She went up to the bedroom and saw that her sister was lying in bed, in a gown watching TV.

"How come you ain't ready, I thought we were going out?"

"You know I'm not taking my big behind out of this house. Nobody wants to see me. Anyway, where is the cake and ice cream that you said you were bringing?"

Carry looked at her watch, "Oh, It's getting delivered. It should be here any moment now." As if they heard her voice the doorbell rang.

"That's it right there. I will go and get it." Carry left out of the room and went down to the living room and opened the door. There were three black men in overcoats standing there. They were all different sizes, with the smallest standing at 5' 5" and the tallest being almost seven feet. They all stepped in and Carry led them to the kitchen she showed them the cake and ice cream, paid them and pointed them to Cara's room. The Mandingo click headed towards Cara's room, while Carry stayed out in the living room.

The lead man opened the bedroom door and they all went in singing happy birthday. Cara looked up surprised by the three black men in her room. She was nervous at first, but then realized that Carry had to be behind it, seeing as they had cake and ice cream in their hands. They sat the cake and ice cream on the dresser. One of them sat a portable stereo on the dresser too. He turned it on and the men took off their coats. They only had on G-strings underneath. When they dropped their coats to the ground, Cara's pussy instantly became wet.

From the smallest to the biggest one they all seemed to have big dicks. Cara knew that her sister had hired them to dance and that they had no interest in her. She figured that she could let them get her hot and finger fuck herself into an orgasm. She slid one of her hands under the cover and started finger fucking herself as she watched them dance. One of the dancers peeped the move and walked over to the bed. He sat on the bed and pulled the cover back. He saw that Cara had her gown up to her waist and did not have any panties on. She had her fat stubby fingers on her pussy. He pulled her hand away.

"What are you doing, it's your birthday. First off what is your name?"

"It's Cara,"

"Second, why are you here alone on your birthday?" Cara started shedding tears as she explained to him.

"My boyfriend left me two years ago and I have no friends."

"Oh, that's too bad, my name is Zeek, and I and my friends are the Mandingo Click. We are going to make sure that you have the best birthday that you can have. Just lay back, relax and let me do this." he told her as he stuck three of his fingers inside of her.

"Gosh your pussy is so wet I must taste your birthday cake." Zeek lowered his head in between Cara's legs and began sucking her pussy. Cara could not believe what was going on. She thought that she had died and gone to heaven the way that he was sucking her pussy. He rose up from her pussy and his lips were coated with pussy juice. His partners quickly joined him over by the bed.

"How is it Zeek?" one of them asked. Zeek turned to face him and he saw how Zeek's mouth was covered with cream.

"I need to get my dick in her." Zed stated. He pulled his dick out of his G-string and asked Cara, "You don't mind if I put this in you do you?" She couldn't believe that she had three fine men crowding around her on her bed. She could not believe that a man was standing in front of her with a dick long as a forearm offering it to her.

"Zeek, Zues, we got to make this a birthday that she won't forget. Let me get some dick into the birthday girl!" Zed said to the others. Zeek got off of the bed and Zed climbed onto it. He positioned himself between her legs and put his dick to her entrance. He tried to force his dick into her, but it wouldn't go. He stuck two of his fingers down there and they easily went in and came out super wet. He said to her, "You're not a virgin, but you must not have had sex in a long time."

"I'm going to need my dick lubed up some more to get inside of you."

The next thing Cara knew, Zed climbed up onto her chest and sat on her humongous titties. He aimed his dick at her mouth, reached out with one of his hands, cuffed her head and lifted it up and put his dick into her mouth. He held her head up, while he started fucking Cara in her mouth.

Cara's mouth was full and her cheeks poked out as he fucked her mouth. As he was fucking her mouth, Zeek had slid his fingers inside of her. He was finger fucking her trying to get her pussy muscles to loosen up. He kept adding fingers until he had all four of them inside of her.

"I think she is ready now." Zeek said to Zed. Zed pulled his dick out of Cara's mouth and climbed back down in between her legs. He lined his dick back up at her entrance and pushed. After some resistance he finally got it in.

"Ah, there we go!" he said once his dick got inside of her.

"I'm going to have my way with this pussy. You don't come across pussy this tight too often. I will tell you, that your boyfriend was a fool to walk away from this pussy." Zed said to Cara. Cara was looking into Zed's eyes as he was fucking her, until she felt a tap on her shoulder. She turned her head and Zues who only stood a little over five feet tall stood at the side of the bed. He was holding a dick in his hand that was as fat as a wrist. He told Cara, "Happy birthday, please enjoy this!" Cara lifted her head up and took his dick into her mouth.

She used her left hand to hold his dick as she sucked it. Someone grabbed her right arm and pulled it behind her, then put her hand on their dick. Zeek put her hand inside of his then wrapped her hand around his dick. He used his hand to move her hand up and down his dick to jack him off. Once he saw that she had caught a rhythm and no longer needed his assistance, he took his hand away.

Zed was in Cara's pussy, Zues had his dick in Cara's mouth and Zeek had his dick in Cara's hand, and Cara loved it. She hadn't felt that good since she had engaged in the threesome with Mike and his friend. Zeek pulled his dick out of her hand and walked over to her dresser. He grabbed a jar of cream and headed back over to the bed.

"Let's all get a hole. I'm tired of being left out." He said to his two partners.

"Zed get on your back and let her get on top of you, you can handle it."

"Zues, hold up!" Zed said to him. Zues pulled his dick out of Cara's mouth. Zed pulled out of Cara then got up off of the bed.

"You two help her up, so that I can get into position. I'm going to turn sideways." They all helped Cara to get up off of the bed and Zeek and Zues held her up while Zed got in position. He laid on his back on the bed, with his legs hanging off the side of it. They helped Cara on top of him. Zeek and Zues held her ass cheeks open, so that Zed could see her pussy hole as they lowered her onto him. Once they lowered Cara onto his dick, Zues ran around to the other side of the bed and got up on it. With his feet firmly planted on the bed he put his hands on the sides of Cara's head and guided his dick into her mouth. Behind her, Zeek scooped some of the cream out of the jar and started rubbing some onto his dick. He also put some onto her asshole. He climbed up on the bed flat footed and put his dick to her asshole entrance. He pushed in until his dick opened her duke shoot up.

Zed was underneath her, holding her ass cheeks open as he kept lifting himself up in her. Zeek was squatting on the bed hitting her in the ass and Zues was in the front fucking her face. Cara was in pain and pleasure, but could only communicate through her body. None of them heard the bed began to crack under all of the weight, the more excited they got the harder they went at it. The bed got to the point that it could not hold all of the weight anymore. The wheels on the rails caved in and the box spring and mattress went crashing to the floor.

Carry, who had dozed off jumped up startled. She ran and busted into her sister's room, "Hey what's going on?" she began as she opened the door. When she got it opened and seen what was going on she did not know how to react. Her sister's bed was on the floor and all three of the dancers were inside of one of her holes.

"What are you guys doing to her?" Zeek looked back and said, "We are giving her a birthday gift." she noticed that Cara had not stopped giving the little guy head. She wanted to know if her sister was alright.

"Cara, are you okay?" Zues pulled his dick from her mouth, and Cara turned her head and said, "Thanks for the birthday present sis!" then she turned back around with her mouth opened, so that Zues could put his dick back into it. Carry left out the room saying to herself, "I hope she looks out for me like that on my birthday."

Clear View

Mathew was a seventeen year old nerdy white boy that lived with his parents in the suburbs of Mayfield Heights, Ohio.

Mathew was a geek and was considered a nerd by everyone that attended his school. Mathew did not care that he did not have any friends. He had a passion for studying the stars and other planets, he loved astronomy.

The only outside activities that Mathew had, was cutting his neighbor Mrs. Harrison's grass on the weekends. Mathew would cut Mrs. Harrison's grass then afterwards she would invite him in and treat him to cookies and milk.

Mrs. Harrison having become a widow three years early at the young age of forty seven lived by herself. She had a grown son that was away, serving in the army. She was lonely and enjoyed chatting with Mathew. She learned early on that he had an obsession for looking out into space. Sometimes at night she would go to her bedroom window and look up to Mathew's window, which was directly across from hers, but was up on the next level. Sometimes she would secretly wish that she was that object that Mathew was watching.

One Saturday, while Mathew was outside cutting her grass, Mrs. Harrison was down in her basement, cleaning it out. While cleaning, she came across her husband's old telescope. She knew that all Mathew had to look out to the sky with was a pair of old binoculars. She figured that she would give him the telescope. She picked it up, carried it upstairs, then went over to the window and called for him to come inside. He yelled back that he was through with the grass and would be in after he put the lawnmower up.

After he put the lawnmower up, Mathew entered the house. He was expecting to see Mrs. Harrison holding a plate of cookies in her hand and a glass of milk, but instead she held a telescope in them. He had been saving up the money that he made from cutting her grass, along with the money that his parents gave him for allowance to purchase him a telescope. He still needed a few hundred dollars to get one, so he was happy when Mrs. Harrison told him, "You can have this. Ed wanted Mark to have it, but he has no interest in the stars, so you can have it." Mathew was beaming as he told her, "Thanks!" He took the Telescope from her hands and headed over to his house.

He took the telescope upstairs and set it up in front of his window. He went and got some towels, some soap and some

Windex. He cleaned the telescope up, and then cleaned the lens. It was still day time, when he got finished and he could not wait for night to fall, so that he could finally get a clear view of the stars. The binoculars only let him see but so far. He pulled out his astronomy book, flopped down on his bed and began reading about the stars that he was planning on seeing that night.

At around ten o'clock that night, Mathew went over to the scope, aimed it at the sky and looked through it. He realized that the focus was blurry and the telescope's lens needed to be adjusted. He pointed the scope downward and began adjusting it. Little did Mathew know that when he pointed the telescope downward he had the scope pointed directly at Mrs. Harrisons' bedroom window.

As he kept adjusting the lens, the picture he was seeing was becoming more and more clear. He was shocked at the picture that he was starting to see. Mrs. Harrison was lying on her bed, completely nude from the waist down. She had her pussy facing Mathew's window, with her legs pulled back and her hand inserting something into her pussy. Mathew adjusted the lens to zoom in and could clearly see that Mrs. Harrison was fucking herself with a large, white dildo.

He raised the scope up to look at her face and seen a look of pure pleasure on it. He readjusted the lens so that he could see her whole body. He watched her fuck herself with the dildo until something shocking happened.

Out of the blue, Mrs. Harrison raised her head up, looked in his direction and smiled. Startled, Mathew quickly backed away from the scope. He waited for a few minutes then went back over to it.

He looked back into it and it was as if Mrs. Harrison was staring him right in his eyes through the scope. She looked in his direction intently, while using one hand to spread her pussy lips open and using her other hand to fuck herself with the dildo feverishly. It was like she was performing just for him. Mathew ran into the bathroom looking for something to masturbate with, and all he could find was some hair conditioner. He ran back into his room, dropped his shorts, lubed his erect dick up with some of the conditioner and put his eye back to the telescope.

Mrs. Harrison was still going at it and he began jacking his dick as he watched her. He saw her making a face that made him wonder if she was cumming. He closed his eyes and fantasized that it was him that was making her cum and he shot his load all over his window sill.

Mathew cleaned his self and his window sill up and went to bed.

The following night at the same time, Mathew went to the scope and pointed it at Mrs. Harrison's window and again she was on her bed fucking herself with the dildo. That time she was in the doggy style position with her ass facing the window. She reached behind and was fucking herself with the dildo from the back. Mathew found himself jacking off again.

The third night it was the same thing only this time Mrs. Harrison was standing at the window, with one foot up on the sill, fucking herself with the dildo. Mathew had found that he had taken enough he couldn't take beating his dick for a third night. He stormed out of his room, downstairs and out of the house.

He rushed over to Mrs. Harrison's house and began pounding on her door. Mrs. Harrison did not know what was going on. She looked up to Mathew's window and could see the scope, but not him. She was hoping that he hadn't given her away to his parents. She threw on her robe, went downstairs and opened the door.

Mathew was standing there with an angry look on his face. Mrs. Harrison tried to dummy up, "Why Mathew what a surprise. How is the telescope working?"

"It works perfectly!" he told her as he stepped in and closed the door behind him.

"It gives me a clear view Mrs. Harrison. A clear view of you fucking yourself with that dildo every night right by the window, so that I can see you and tonight it stops, you are not going to keep antagonizing me!" Mrs. Harrison was blown away by his cockiness.

He did not seem like a nerd at all. He stepped to her, undid the tie on her robe and it fell open.

"Just as I thought!"

"I'm sorry Mathew I am old and have just been lonely. I did not mean to cause you any harm."

"There is nothing to be sorry about Mrs. Harrison, but I do intend to do you harm." he told her as he began taking off his pajama bottoms. Mrs. Harrison stood there looking shocked, for a young boy she seen that Mathew had a huge cock. His dick was sticking straight up in the air. He walked over to Mrs. Harrison and helped her out of her robe. He led her over to the kitchen table and told her, "Please assume the position Mrs. Harrison." she leaned over and placed her hands on the table and said, "Please be gentle with me, it has been awhile." Mathew went up behind her and guided his dick into her pussy.

"Oooh!" Mrs. Harrison purred as he put his dick inside of her. Mathew put his hands onto her waist and started fucking her. Mrs. Harrison was moaning and groaning while he was fucking her.

"Doesn't this feel much better than a piece of rubber Mrs. Harrison?" he asked her.

"Oh, Mathew it feels so much better. I haven't felt this good since Ed was alive."

"Put your leg up on the chair." he told her and Mrs. Harrison put one of her legs up onto a kitchen chair. That position gave Mathew better access to invade her pussy. Mathew was fucking Mrs. Harrison and she told him, "Oh my Oh dear that feels so good!" Mathew told her, "After all that you put me through, you must suck my cock, have a seat in the chair."

She sat in the chair and started giving him head. He busted off in her mouth and they called it a night. Mathew kept on fucking Mrs. Harrison and the more he fucked her, the more confidence he gained.

He no longer wore glasses, he wore contacts instead. He gained a sense of confidence from fucking Mrs. Harrison that it turned him from a geek to a stud. Everyone at school noticed his transformation especially the girls, who started flocking to him. Ever since Mathew had started fucking Mrs. Harrison all the girls wanted to give him a clear view of their goods.

Speaks No English

Marcus was a college student majoring in Computer engineering. One of his classes was computer graphics. One day Marcus entered the class ten minutes late. He entered with his head down, rushed to his seat and sat down. When he sat down the professor called out to him, "Mr. Smith I'm glad that you could join us." Marcus raised his head to look up front at the professor and seen the most beautiful Chinese girl that he had ever seen in his life.

He had never seen her before and wondered why she was standing up front with the professor. He did not have to wait long to find out.

"As I was telling the rest of the class Mr. Smith, this here is Sue Lynn and she is an exchange student. Ms. Lynn knows very little English, so I want you guys to show her our American hospitality, by being as helpful as you can to her.

Mr. Smith since you were late without an excuse, I am making it your job to show Ms. Lynn around the campus today. Make sure she learns her way to all of her classrooms as well as the cafeteria."

Marcus had a girl on campus that he had been trying to get with forever and she had just agreed the day before to have lunch with him that day. He was not trying to mess up his chance with Samantha, by having to play chaperone to some girl that could not even speak English.

He raised his hand in order to protest the professor assigning him as the chaperone. The professor knew what he wanted and told him, "Mr. Smith, this is not up for a debate. If you do not want to accept the assignment, then you can do a two thousand word essay explaining why you were late to my class for the third time in two months."

Marcus put his hand down and let out a deep breath. There was no way that he was going to write a two thousand word essay, "There goes my chance with Samantha." he said to himself.

The professor spoke to the student that was sitting in the chair next to Marcus, "Ms. Williams could you move to another seat please, to allow Ms. Lynn to sit next to Mr. Smith?"

The student got up and moved to another chair and the professor said some words to Sue Lynn while pointing in Marcus' direction. Sue Lynn looked at Marcus and smiled then headed in his direction. They locked eyes all the way until she got to her seat. Sue Lynn was staring into Marcus' eyes so hard that he thought she could see inside his soul. When she got next to him she smiled again and he could see the dimples in her cheeks. She set down beside him and class started.

When the bell rung and it was time to go to their next class, Marcus got up and started walking out of the class. Sue Lynn got up and started following him. When they got into the hallway Marcus turned to her and asked her what was her next class. She just stood there staring at him, not understanding what he was saying. Marcus pulled his school schedule out and showed it to her. Sue Lynn smiled, reached into her pocket, pulled out her schedule and handed it to Marcus. He took it, looked at it then handed it back to her.

He took off walking with her following him. As they were walking someone called his name. He stopped and Sue Lynn bumped into him. She was startled and just stood there. Marcus looked over her shoulder and saw Samantha coming their way. Sue Lynn turned around to see why they had stopped and seen Samantha coming their way also. Once Samantha got to them she looked Sue Lynn up and down, and then turned to Marcus, "Are we still on for lunch?" Marcus blew out a long breath, and then told her, "Yes but, unfortunately she has to come along." he told her pointing to Sue Lynn.

"And who is she?"

"She is an exchange student, and because I was late to class Professor Macklin assigned me to be her chaperone for today." Samantha looked at Sue Lynn again. She took in how pretty she was. Sue Lynn noticed how she looked at her and frown at her.

"Chaperone huh, well see me when you don't have any excessive baggage." Samantha said to him then walked away. Marcus knew he had blown his chance with her. He took off again, showing Sue Lynn to her English class. He dropped her off at class then went to his class. He sat in his class but his mind was somewhere else. He was daydreaming about Sue Lynn and how pretty she was. He wished that she knew English so that they could communicate.

He has never been with someone from another race and thought that having a Chinese girlfriend might be cool. He came to his senses when the bell rang. He knew that he had no chance with Sue Lynn. She was an exchange student plus she could not speak English, so they could not even communicate with each other.

He left his class and headed to pick her up from her class. When he got to her class, Sue Lynn was standing outside of it. She smiled when she seen him coming. When he got to her, she threw her arms around him and hugged him. Marcus was shocked by her actions and quickly pulled away from her. Sue Lynn frowned when he pulled away.

"Let's go eat." he said to her and they took off walking. He walked for a minute then realized that she wasn't with him. He turned and seen that she was still standing by her English class with her arms folded across her chest.

Marcus walked back and said again to her, "Let's go eat!" Sue Lynn just looked at him. He took his hand and acted like he was feeding himself trying to get her to understand what he was saying. When she acted as if she still did not understand him, he grabbed her hand and led her to the cafeteria. When they got to the cafeteria, he led her into the line and asked her what she wanted to eat. She indicated that she wanted the burger that she saw being advertised up on the board. Marcus ordered for both of them and they went and sat at a table. They sat in chairs that were across from each other, until Sue Lynn got up and moved her chair over next to Marcus' chair. She took one of her French fries and put it up to his mouth and he bit it.

Sue Lynn started to giggle and fed him another fry. Marcus started to loosen up. He started thinking that chaperoning her around might not be so bad after all.

He reached over and grabbed one of her fries and fed it to her. Instead of biting it, she sucked it into her mouth. The way she slurped it in, seemed like a sexual gesture to Marcus. He fed her another one and she slurped it in again then licked around her lips. Marcus found himself getting hard. He looked at Sue Lynn, who stared into his eyes as she put her hand under the table and grabbed his dick. Marcus jumped hitting the table causing everything to rattle.

Sue Lynn pulled her hand back and giggled. Marcus had to wait for his hard on to go down so that he could get up and dump their trash.

After he dumped their trash they headed out of the cafeteria to head to their next class. Sue Lynn seen the picture of a lady on a door and knew that it was a restroom, and she indicated to Marcus that she needed to use it. Marcus stopped by the bathroom intending to wait on her to handle her business. He was surprised when she grabbed his hand and snatched him into the bathroom with her. He did not know what she was up to, but it did not take long to find out. She led him into a stall and locked it. She sat down on the toilet and said, "Si si" pointing at Marcus' dick. She reached out with her hand, grabbed his zipper and started pulling it down.

Marcus could not believe what was going on. He looked on in shock as Sue Lynn pulled his dick out and started playing doctor with it. She gave it a full examination, even feeling the weight of his balls in her hands. After the examination she grabbed his dick with one hand then lowered her mouth onto it. Marcus looked down and seen that she had her eyes closed as she was sucking his dick. The feeling was so good that he had to spread his arms out. He put one on the wall and one on the stall's divider.

It was all that he could do to keep from losing his balance. The head that Sue Lynn was giving him was throwing his equilibrium off. All of a sudden Sue Lynn stopped sucking his dick and stood up. She reached under her skirt and pulled her colorful panties off.

"Sit!" she said to Marcus pointing at the toilet. Marcus sat on the toilet and Sue Lynn lifted her right leg and put it onto his shoulder, "Eat!" she said. Marcus thought to himself, "For a girl that don't know much English, she sure knows the words she needs to use to get what she wants."

First he played in her pussy hairs. They were thick, jet black and very straight. They looked pretty all by themselves. After he played in her hairs, he commenced to eating her pussy. Sue Lynn was enjoying the feeling that he was giving her. She put her hands on the sides of his head to keep her balance, while she kept her leg up on his shoulder. Marcus had never had any Chinese pussy and just knowing that he was getting it, he started performing as if he was up for a Grammy award.

Sue Lynn's left leg started shaking and Marcus had to put his hand on her waist to keep her from falling as she started cumming.

"Me cum! Me cumming!" she said as her body started shaking wildly. Her hands were shaking on his head causing him to shake too. Now that she had cum and Marcus had got his nut, he thought that it was over. Sue Lynn took her leg off of his shoulder then pulled him up off of the toilet. He got up then she climbed up on top of the toilet bowl, squatted down, then turned her head back to him and said, "Kitty, you get!" Marcus understood perfectly clear and eased up behind her and guided his dick into her. Sue Lynn stuck her arms out and used them to brace herself on the back wall as Marcus started to pound her pussy. Marcus pushed her skirt up onto her back and seen that she had a tattoo of a dragon on the small of her back.

He was loving the firmness of her small, round ass. What really got him was when he looked down to watch his dick go in and out of her, he seen his dick coated with thick white cream. Sue Lynn was moaning and panting. She kept bending her legs in then pushing them out to meet his thrust. When she felt like she was about to cum she yelled to him, "Bang! You bang!" Marcus started pounding Sue Lynn's pussy like she wanted it and when he felt her pussy cream all over his dick it ignited him and he shot his load into her.

Marcus was so exhausted that he had to sit down on the stall's floor for a minute to catch his breath. He sat there thinking, "This is the most unbelievable day of my life."

Sue Lynn pulled her skirt down and pulled her panties up, then she looked down at Marcus and said, "You better hurry before you be late for your next class." then she smiled. She stepped over Marcus and left out of the stall headed to her next class. Marcus jumped up and started to hurry putting his clothes back on so that he could get out of there. He did not know what would happen if he got caught inside of the girl's restroom.

"Maybe they will make me into another chaperone." he said to himself smiling as he walked out of the restroom.

Age Ain't Nothing but a Number

Evelynn had gotten off of work on a Friday evening and wanted to go and have a few drinks to wind down. She chose to go to the bar, which was a twenty-five and up bar. It had a laid back atmosphere because there weren't too many people from the hip hop culture there, because of the dress code.

On Fridays no jeans or tennis shoes were allowed. She also liked the fact that they played mostly R&B and Jazz on Fridays.

Evelynn was sitting at the bar, sipping on her drink, when a guy that did not even look to be twenty-five sat on the stool next to her. She looked at him and noticed that he barely had any facial hair. She looked down and seen that he had on some Bugle Boy khakis and a pair of soft sole shoes. She could tell that he did just what was necessary to get in.

A song by the OJay's came on and Evelynn started dancing in her seat. Terrance turned and looked at her, sitting on the stool moving her upper body. He liked the way that her titties were bouncing as she moved and popped her fingers. He looked down to her waist area and saw how her ass was hanging off the sides of the stool.

"Baby got back!" he thought to himself. Terrance was only twenty-three and only got into the club because his uncle Melvin was the bouncer at the door. Terrance always went to the Mirage on Fridays. For some reason he did not like attending the rowdy hip hop clubs, plus he did not like the young girls that only seemed to be sack chasers.

Terrance had been going to the Mirage for a while in hopes of finding an older, more mature woman. He had met a couple that got drunk, took him home and had sex with him. None of them had the air of a diva about themselves. They were all washed up.

Terrance looked at Evelynn sitting on her stool nursing her drink and could tell that she had some pizazz about herself.

The way she sat with her back straight showed that she had confidence in herself and the fact that she was buying her own drinks showed that she was independent.

Another song came on and he seen how she started tapping her foot on the floor.

"It's worth a try." he said to himself then turned and asked her, "Excuse me but would you like to dance?" Evelynn heard him say something and turned her stool around so that she could face him.

"What did you say?" she asked him.

"Would you like to dance?" Evelynn laughed and he got offended.

"What's so funny?" he asked. She just stared at him for a moment. To be young, he did look sexy to her and he definitely had the body of a man. She looked down at his finger nails and saw that they were clean. She looked back up to his face and seen that he was staring at her.

"How old are you?" she asked him.

"I'm almost twenty-four." Evelynn laughed again then said, "I'm over twice your age."

"What does that matter, you have been dancing with yourself for the last three songs, and I'm offering to dance with you." Evelyn was taken aback at how intent he was and the fact that he wasn't intimidated by her like most men were.

"I don't dance like those models in the videos."

"Neither do I, now could we go dance?" he asked her while sticking his hand out. Evelynn took his hand and he led her to the dance floor.

They danced off of Cameo's song *Like Candy*. The way that Terrance was dancing, allowed Evelyn to see that he had an old soul. He wasn't dancing like the young, teeny boppers.

The song ended and the slow song *In Between the Sheets* by the Isley Brothers began playing. Evelynn was surprised when Terrance grabbed her hand and started hand dancing with her. He had good rhythm and knew all of the moves. He spun Evelynn around, so that she faced away from him, then pulled her to him and put his arms around her waist. He pressed himself up against her and their bodies moved as one to the beat.

Terrance held her so close that she could feel his dick print on her ass. When he put his face on the side of hers, she could smell the Cool Water Cologne that he had on. Terrance held her tightly as he grinded his dick on her ass. When he breathed, his hot breath hit Evelyn's neck.

She started feeling sensual and began grinding her ass back on his dick. She could not believe how that young boy had her feeling. Terrance turned her around so that they were facing each other. He put his hands onto the small of her back and began to grind on her.

Evelyn could feel his hard dick in her pelvis area. Her titties got hard as they rubbed against his chest.

All of a sudden, Terrance dropped his hands to her ass and gripped her cheeks. He squeezed them as he danced with her. Evelynn closed her eyes and began to forget that she was on the dance floor as she grinded her pussy up against his dick. Terrance whispered in her ear, "Let me make this the best night of your life." Evelynn thought to herself, "Look at this young boy trying to put his game down on me. He probably ain't nothing but a wham bam thank you ma'am type of boy."

The song ended and she broke away from him and headed back to her seat. Terrance followed her with his dick still hard as a rock. She climbed back up on her seat and Terrance stood in front of her.

They locked eyes for a moment and Terrance asked her, "Let me make love to you?" With lust in her eyes, Evelynn looked at him and asked, "What do your young ass know about making love? I don't need no two minute man or a hard fuck. I can do that my damn self!" Terrance remained cool and responded, "Don't let my age fool you. When I'm done with you your body will crave for me like a drug." Evelynn thought to herself, "Damn, he talk a good game. I wonder can he live up to it. Fuck it, you only live once."

She looked at Terrance, smiled and said, "I'm going to see what your young ass is really about, let's go." Terrance grabbed her hand, helped her off of the stool and they headed outside.

"Do you have your own car?" Evelynn asked him.

"I ride a bike."

"He is riding a bike, Lord what have I gotten myself into, fuck it there is no turning back now," she looked at Terrance, "Will it fit into my trunk?"

"It's not that type of bike. It's a motorcycle. It's a eleven hundred Suzuki."

"Oh, Okay you can follow me then."

"I will get my bike and meet you back here." They went their separate ways and met back up. Evelynn pulled out the lot driving her Lexus GS 400, with Terrance following her. When she stopped at a red light he pulled up alongside of her and when the light turned green he took off raising his bike into a wheelie.

Evelynn trailed behind him thinking that he was going to kill himself. When they got to the next light, she rolled her window down and told him that, and for the rest of the way Terrance rode behind her without doing any tricks.

They got to Evelyn's house and he pulled into the driveway behind her. He got off of his bike and Evelynn led him into her house. They both knew what they had come there for, so Evelynn bypassed the living room and headed straight up to her bedroom.

Once inside, she turned on her miniature stereo system and her television. She had gone to the bar straight from work, so she wanted to freshen up. She grabbed a gown out of her drawer, told Terrance to make his self comfortable, and headed to the bathroom to take a shower.

Terrance was a spontaneous person. He stripped out of his clothes and headed out into the hallway butt naked in search of the bathroom. He followed the sound of the shower and opened the bathroom door. He stepped in, closed the door then went over to the tub. He slid the shower curtain open and Evelynn opened her eyes. She was shocked but couldn't say anything because she was mesmerized by his body.

With his clothes on she couldn't tell the he had all the muscles that were bulging out. She looked down at his dick and thought back to him grinding it on her at the club. She thought, "He must of had it balled up like a fist, because I sure couldn't tell that it was that big."

Terrance stepped into the shower and took the soap and rag out of her hand. He stood facing her and began washing her body. He washed her titties lifting them up and getting underneath them. He washed her stomach then slid the washcloth down to her pussy.

Evelyn squatted a little so that he could get up in there. The way he washed her pussy was sensual and Evelynn found herself getting hot.

When he got through with her front he reached around and started washing her back. He washed her ass cheeks and in between her ass. He sat down on the tub and put her foot up on his thigh. He washed both of her calves and feet.

After washing Evelynn he had her rinse off, and then they got out of the shower where he grabbed a towel and dried her off. Terrance picked her up and carried her to the bedroom.

Once they were in the bedroom, he laid her face down onto the bed. He straddled her back and began giving her a massage, starting at her neck. His hands felt so soothing to Evelynn. He dug the tips of his fingers into her neck and started moving them in a circular motion. He dug his thumbs into the base of her neck.

Evelynn started feeling so relieved. She never even knew she had that much tension inside of her until he started releasing it. He did her shoulders and her back. He used his knuckles to knead them into her back. He massaged every part of her body, her ass cheeks, her calves and her feet.

Evelynn could not believe how he had her feeling, most men twice his age did not have the patience to do the things that he was doing to her. He had her leg bent back massaging her foot, when the next thing she knew she felt a warm sensation on her big toe. She turned her head and looked back and saw that Terrance had her toe in his mouth sucking on it. She seen that his eyes was closed and from the look on his face she knew that he was enjoying what he was doing. The feeling felt so good to her.

After that he spread her legs apart, pulled her hips up off of the bed and started sucking her pussy from the back. He took his thumbs and separated her ass cheeks, giving himself good access to her pussy. He licked it, sucked it and nibbled on it.

Evelyn's eyes rolled into the back of her head and her eye lids fluttered as she enjoyed the feeling that he was giving her. He ate her until she came. She felt fulfilled, which she had not felt like in a while. She was good with that one nut, but the show was just getting started. Terrance rose up and slid his dick into her from the back. He sunk all the way into her and laid on top of her. He whispered in her ear, "This is where it gets real good. Feel how this young boy gives it to you." he started pulling out slowly then sinking back into her. He held her ass cheeks open and started giving her his dick. The feeling was so good that Evelynn grabbed a pillow and started biting into it.

"Evelynn your pussy feels so good. It is so hot and wet. You are like fine wine you only get better with time. Show me that you like it, give it back to me. Come on baby give me that pussy."

Evelynn didn't know what was going on. He had her in bliss. She pushed back and got up, because she wanted him to fuck her doggy style. She wanted him to get his dick further up in her. Terrance rose up allowing her to get in the doggy style position. He took his hands off of her ass and put them on her waist.

"Is it good to you?"

"I'm I lasting?"

"Don't talk just show me with your body." Evelyn started rocking on her knees and rotating her hips. She even started talking back, "Damn, your young ass feel so good. Your dick feels so good. You showed me that you are a man that you can make love. I need to be fucked now. Put it on me makes me regret that I doubted you." Evelynn reached back with her hands to spread her ass cheeks open for him and he started pounding her.

He got up onto his feet in a squatting position and fucked her like a beast. He was sweating and the sweat dripped from his forehead onto her back. He took his hand and put them under her, grabbing her titties. He squeezed them as he continued to pound her pussy.

"That's it baby fuck this pussy. Damn I need it like this all the time. Terrance took his hands off of her titties and put them on her ankles. He pulled her ankles straightening out her legs and making her fall back onto her stomach. He put his hands on her knees and stood up on the bed. Her bottom half of her body was raised off the bed. He had her in the wheel barrow position. She put her hands down on the bed and pushed herself up to aid him in fucking the shit out of her.

"This is it!" he said to her then started skeeting in her. She felt his dick pulsate as he was shooting his nut inside of her, which triggered another orgasm for her. They both were tired and fell onto the bed lying side by side.

Terrance was feeling good, because he knew that he had put in some real work. He got dressed and before he left him and Evelynn exchanged numbers. He promised to come back the next day and take her for a ride on his bike, she escorted him out of the house and he got on his bike. When he pulled out of her driveway, he lifted his bike and did a wheelie all the way to the end of the street.

Evelynn went straight to the phone, even though it was the middle of the night she had to tell her friend what had happened. She dialed Cynthia's number and it rang ten times before she picked it up. Groggily Cynthia asked, "Who is this?"

"Girl, it's me Evelynn, I had to call you and tell you what happened to me tonight."

"It better be something good or I know what is going to happen to your ass, waking me up out of my sleep and shit."

"Girl, I went to the Mirage and met a young boy that put it on me?" Cynthia perked up.

"How old was he?"

"Twenty-three,"

"Bitch he is a kid, he ain't do shit!"

"Hoe, after what he did to me, can't nobody tell me shit. He made me a firm believer that age ain't nothing but a number."

Just another Day at Work

It was just another day at work for Mary. She sat looking at her computer screen bored. She was looking at the long list of people that she was going to have to call and harass that day. Mary worked for a telemarketing firm and was fed information through her computer that told her who to call and how much they owed to a certain company.

To Mary, her job was boring. She did not understand why companies spent so much money to have people call other people to remind them that they owed the company money. As if the people did not already know that they owed the company.

Instead of calling and harassing people sometimes Mary would just sit in front of her computer screen and fantasize about Dave, who was her shift supervisor.

Dave's job was to make sure that the workers were doing their job. Sometimes workers would get bored with their job and do things like surf the internet or play games on their computers. Dave would randomly tap into the employee's computers or eavesdrop on their phone calls to make sure that they were doing their jobs.

His office was in a position where he could watch the whole floor. Some of the worker's workstations faced his office and they could look directly into it. Mary was one of those workers and sometimes she would look into Dave's office and stare at him as she masturbated.

Mary was kind of homely looking. She was about twenty pounds overweight, had long greasy hair and a few pimples on her face. Mary thought that the pimples came from her lack of sex. The only sex that Mary got was from either her fingers or her trusted vibrator, that she named Homerun.

Mary stayed horny and sometimes would masturbate two or three times a day. Actually Mary was addicted to masturbation and would often masturbate at work while sitting at her computer.

Dave was often the person that she would fantasize about, while she finger fucked herself to an orgasm. To her he was a sex God. Dave stood six feet tall, and was slim with an athletic body. He had blond hair with mesmerizing blue eyes.

Every time that Mary would see him her pussy would instantly get wet. She had a dream at home one night that Dave had called her into his office, after a virus had crippled the computers. They were going over the list of people that he had printed out for her to call, when the next thing she knew, Dave had her bent over the desk fucking her from behind.

This day at work, Mary used that dream to finger fuck herself to a nut. She had no panties on and she hiked her skirt up in the front, spread her legs and looked over top of her station at Dave while she fucked herself. Because of the dividers between their work stations, no one knew what Mary was doing.

Dave seen Mary staring at him and knew that she must have been doing what she often did while at her work station, which was masturbating. There were many times that Dave had locked eyes with Mary and knew that she was doing something that she was not supposed to be doing. Sometimes he would catch her with her eyes closed, with a look of pleasure on her face. He knew that she had to be masturbating and often wondered who the object of her desire was. He thought that she would be looking at sexual images on her computer.

To Dave, Mary was sexy. He liked chunky girls, and if it wasn't for the few pimples that she had on her face he thought that she would be beautiful. He had read an article on the things that causes a grown person to have pimples there were three main things the type of diet, the type of soap or cream that one used or the lack of sex.

Dave often wondered which one it was that caused Mary the bumps. Dave had jacked off many times at work, while watching Mary. When she would have her eyes closed making fuck faces, Dave would become aroused and pull his dick out of his slacks. He would jack his dick under his desk to the looks that Mary would have on her face, fantasizing that it was him that was causing the faces that she would make.

This day Dave's dick instantly got hard when the aroused look appeared on Mary's face. He decided that he was tired of playing the little games and that he was not going to sit around any longer and let her get off to sexual images on her computer. She didn't have to use images, when he would eagerly give her what she needed.

He got up from his desk and realized that his hard on was showing, so he grabbed a file off of his desk and used it to shield his hard on. He left his office and headed over to Mary's workstation. Mary had her eyes closed and was about to cum when Dave called out her name, "Mary!" Mary was cumming and could not control herself. Her body was shaking and she had to wait for it to stop, for her to pull her fingers from her pussy and to pull her skirt down.

She turned and looked at Dave and by her sitting down she became face to face with his crotch area. She could see that he had a hard on, even though he was trying to hide it with the file that he held in his hand. With a flushed face she answered him, "Yes Mr. Barnes?" Dave was very observant and saw that there were no sexual images on her screen. He did however see that she was definitely masturbating. He watched as she pulled her skirt down and he saw the cream on her fingers.

In a professional voice Dave told Mary, "I need to see you to stay behind after work, we have to talk."

"Okay, Mr. Barnes." she said nervously.

All day Mary sat wondering what she had done, or what he had caught her doing. She did not think he had actually caught her masturbating. If he did she was sure that she was about to lose her job. She figured that she would just have to wait until after work to find out.

Five o'clock came and the workers started clocking out and filing out of work. Mary sat at her desk waiting for Dave to call her into his office.

Dave escorted the last worker out of the office then walked back towards his. When he got to his office he called for Mary to step in. Mary nervously got up from her workstation and headed to Dave's office. When she got there, Dave was sitting behind his desk.

"Mary come on in and close the door and have a seat." Mary did as she was told and when she sat down she crossed her legs and her short skirt rose up to the middle of her thighs. Dave enjoyed the view, as they sat there in silence for a few moments which was killing Mary.

"So Mary, how are things going for you?" The question caught Mary off guard and she did not really know how to respond to it.

"Uh, I'm fine Mr. Barnes."

"How is your sex life?"

"Excuse me?"

"Come now Mary, you think that I don't know that you be over there masturbating at your station?"

"Mr. Barnes I … I,"

"You don't have to explain. It's evident that you are not being tended it to, by those pimples that are covering your forehead. You know, I often sat here wondering what was helping you to reach those climaxes. I really thought that you were looking at sexual images on your computer. When I came to your station today, I truly thought that I would find some type of sexual content being shown on your computer, but there wasn't any. May I ask you what do you sit there and fantasize about while you masturbate?"

"Mr. Barnes, am I going to be fired?"

"Definitely not, just be honest with me and we will resolve this matter just between us."

"It be you Mr. Barnes."

"That's what I figured. Why couldn't you just come tell me that you were attracted to me?"

"Look at me, I'm overweight and I'm not good at taking rejections."

"Mary you are a beautiful young lady, and I think that I got a cure for clearing up those pimples on your face. You don't know how many times that I have jacked my dick to the looks that you had on your face. My dick is so hard right now that it is about to bust." Dave said to her as he stood up.

Mary saw the print of his dick trying to bust through his pants. It looked to be as thick as a wrist and as long as a ruler and she started to get very nervous as he walked towards her. He unzipped his pants and pulled his dick out as he walked toward her. Mary found that her mouth was starting to water. I have to have my dick in your mouth Mary. Your lips are so full and luscious and it is as if they were made for dick sucking."

Dave held his dick in his hand as he stood in front of Mary, who hesitated for a minute before she reached out with her hand and stroked his dick. She had to touch it to make sure that it was really real, because she had never in her life seen a dick as big as Dave's. She leaned her head forward and took Dave into her mouth.

"Ah, yes my dear, that's it!" he said to her as she sucked his dick. He took his fingers and ran them through her hair. Mary hungrily sucked on his dick. She could not believe that he was allowing her to suck him off, so she intended to make the best of it just in case it never happened again. She sucked his dick and licked his balls until he almost couldn't take it anymore.

"That is enough my dear. I must get inside of you. He grabbed Mary's hand and lifted her out of her seat and led her over to his desk, pulled her skirt up above her waist and helped her up on his desk.

"No panties!" he said as he spread her legs.

"My God your pussy is so fat I have to suck on these lips." Dave lowered his head in between her legs, and took one of his fingers to separate her pussy lips. He took one of her lips into his mouth and began sucking on it. Ripples of pleasure went through Mary's body. The heat from his breath felt so good to her. He sucked her other lip, then stuck his tongue into her pussy and licked around the inside. Mary could not be still and did not know what to do with her hands, so she placed them on his head.

"Oh God Mr. Barnes, you are about to suck the life out of me." Dave went crazy sucking on Mary's pussy. He brought her to an orgasm that caused her to raise her ass completely up off of the desk. After her orgasm subsided, Dave stood up and guided his dick to her entrance. He put the head to the entrance and pushed in. Mary's pussy was the tightest that he had ever been in. She was as close to a virgin as one could get. Mary sighed from the pleasure as he sunk into her. Dave looked down at how her pussy was clinging to his dick.

"This is a perfect fit, doesn't this feel better than fucking yourself?"

"Oh yes! Yes!" Dave hit her with long strokes, as he pushed her blouse up and pulled her titties out of her bra. He massaged and gripped her titties as he fucked her.

"So wet so tender, I love fucking you Mary. How could you keep this fat, meaty pussy from me? From here on out it has to be me, no more fingers or foreign objects. I must keep this dick in you." Dave talking to Mary sent her overboard and she came to another climax.

After she climaxed for the second time, Dave helped her down off of the desk and had her get on her knees.

"We must see if my anecdote works at clearing up your face." Dave told her then began jacking his dick.

"Oh shit get ready, here it comes. Here it come Mary!" Dave held his dick aiming it at Mary's face. His nut was coming so powerful, that he rose up on his toes and started skeeting his nut all over Mary's face. Mary loved it, and did not even close her eyes. Cum hit her on every part of her face. Dave used his hand to jack the cum out of his dick onto Mary's face.

"You must rub it in dear, get it into your skin." Mary rubbed the semen all over her face. She even took her finger, scooped up some and stuck it into her mouth. She loved the taste of Dave.

That day was the beginning of a relationship that would last for a long time. Dave and Mary entered into a relationship that included them having sex at least three times a week. Miraculously by the second week, Mary's face had started to clear up. They did not know if it was from the sex altogether or the nut facial packs that he would give her.

Because Dave was her supervisor they kept their relationship on the low and stopped having sex at work. Mary never forgot how just another day at work had turned into the best day of her life.

A Little Cream In Our Coffee

Tonya and Judy were sitting up in Jack's bar vibing to the music. Jack's was a neighborhood bar that catered to the hip hop crowd. The ballers and want-to-be ballers attended Jack's every Monday, Wednesday and Sunday.

Most of the girls that attended Jacks were either looking for a good time or trying to catch the attention of the supposed to be ballers.

Tonya and Judy came to Jack's to have a good time. They were both fed up with messing around with the so called ballers. Judy sat on her bar stool looking around the bar with a disgusted look on her face. She had bought herself a couple of doubles of Hennessy and had taken it straight to the head. She was lightweight feeling the effects of her drinks as she looked around the bar.

She started talking to Tonya, "Look at all these sorry ass niggas with their fake balling ass. If they weren't getting any money, half of them wouldn't even be getting any pussy." Tonya had witnessed Judy go into that type of tantrum before. She had been through it many times before. For some reason, Judy had become real bitter towards black men or at least the want-to-be baller black men.

"Judy girl what are you tripping on now?"

"I'm tripping on these fake mother fuckers, up in here acting like they are all of that, when most of them can't even make a bitch cum."

"Why do you have us constantly come up in here, just so that you can get drunk and rant and rave?"

"You know what, let's go I'm tired of these tired ass niggas. I want to go to a white bar."

"Bitch! What can a little dick white boy do for your big behind."

"Don't fall for that myth all them white boys don't got little dicks. Best of all they don't have to have material things to feel good about themselves. I'm just tired of these niggas getting a little money and thinking that they are the shit, when they can't fuck or hardly eat pussy. I'm ready to try me a white boy seriously."

"So, you know where a white club is at?"

"We can go downtown there are a lot of white clubs down there, are you willing to go with me?"

"You are a crazy bitch, but you are my girl. If you want to go to a white bar, then I am with you."

Judy and Tonya left Jack's bar. They got into Judy's car and she headed downtown. Judy drove down to the flats, which was filled with all types of clubs and bars. She drove around until she came to a bar called Larry's and pulled into the parking lot.

"With a name like Larry's this has got to be a white people's bar." she said to Tonya as she pulled into a parking spot. She cut the car off and they both got out and headed to the bar. When they got to the door they had to pay a five dollar cover charge.

They entered the bar and they thought they were at a rodeo event. The inside of the bar looked like a corral. There was even a mechanical bull inside. Most of the customers had on jeans, plaid shirts and cowboy boots.

There was a big dance floor and a lot of people were out there line dancing. Judy and Tonya went over to the bar and ordered drinks. After they got their drinks, they turned their backs to the bar and observed the club. It wasn't hard for them to see that they were the only two blacks in the club.

Even though they were the only blacks inside, they didn't feel any tension. Everybody seemed to be having fun and paid them no attention.

"Look at them, no bling bling, no bottles of Ciroc or Cristal. They are just having a good time. No pants hanging off of their asses. With those tight jeans that they have on, it won't be hard to spot the big dick ones. Matter of fact lets join them on the dance floor." Judy said to Tonya.

"Bitch! I don't know how to do no country line dancing."

"Girl come on, it can't be that hard." Judy grabbed Tonya's hand and led her out to the dance floor. They got out there and found that the moves that they were doing wasn't as simple as they thought they would be. Judy and Tonya found themselves off beat and out of sync with everyone else.

A white guy appeared next to Judy, "You need help learning the moves?" Judy looked up into a set of eyes that were bluer than the Mediterranean Sea. She started at the top of his head, taking in his cowboy hat, she saw the rusty blond hair that hung out of it. She took in his face, which to her was fine even with his long thin nose. Next she took in his upper body, which looked very athletic. Last she went below his waist, taking in his crotch area. Her eyes got wide as she thought to herself, "This hillbilly done had the nerve to stuff something down the front of his pants."

She just knew that it was not all him poking out of those jeans like that. Then she thought, "Maybe I will find out." she spoke to him, "Yeah you can help us, this is our first time."

"Well my name is Ted, and I would love to teach you two how we dance in here." Ted showed Judy and Tonya the moves and before the song was over they were in sync with everyone else.

After the song was over, both Judy and Tonya were tired and went back over to the bar to nurse their drink.

"These white people be dancing their asses off." Judy said to Tonya.

"Yeah, they ass dance just as much as we do."

"You disappeared on me sugar." Judy turned around and Ted was standing there. He had another guy standing behind him.

"We were tired and needed to take a break."

"Well, this is my friend Ronnie and we see that you are here alone and we just want to show you some hospitality."

"This is my friend Tonya."

"Hey there Tonya," Ronnie said anxiously to her. Tonya looked at Ronnie and realized that he reminded her of Opie off of the Andy Griffith show.

"Hi Ronnie!" she said to him.

"So, what made you two decide to come in here?" Ted asked Judy.

"We are just looking for a change we got tired of doing the same thing over and over."

"So did you come just to enjoy yourself or to meet someone?"

"Well a little of both."

"Well, you two have met us and you have enjoyed yourself. How about we move the party somewhere else?" Ted asked.

"Like where?"

"A motel room," Judy started giggling.

"One thing for sure you are not shy. I don't know about no hotel. Have you guys ever been with black women before?"

"No, sure haven't." Ted told her. Ronnie was too embarrassed by the question. He blushed and nodded his head indicating that he had not.

"Do you think that y'all can handle us?" Judy asked them.

"The question is will you two be able to handle us." Ted said as he grabbed his dick. Both Judy and Tonya looked at him holding his dick in his hand and neither of them could believe that it was his dick.

Judy being the boldest out of the two reached out and grabbed his dick and squeezed it. It wasn't even hard, yet it filled her hand.

"Damn!" Was all she could say.

"Are you fillies ready to go?" Ted asked them. Judy looked at Tonya then told them, "We will follow you in my car."

They all got into their cars and Judy followed them to the Western Inn. They got out and walked to the motel's office. Everyone stood outside while Ted went in and paid for the room. When he came out Judy asked him, "Did you get two rooms?"

"I got adjoining rooms." They headed to the room. Ted opened the door and they entered. Inside of the room was a door that led to the connecting room. Ted opened it and said, "That there room is for Ronnie and your friend. Ronnie stood there turning red. Tonya thought that he looked cute with his freckles. She thought that it was going to be funny turning out Andy Griffith's son. She grabbed his hand and led him to the other room and pulled the door closed behind them.

"Well Missy, are you ready to have a good time?"

"I hope you are not a minute man?"

"I have broken in many fillies, but I never broke one in that fast. Just tell me how you want it. You want me to take my time and make love to you or do you want me to fuck you royally?"

"You have a lot of confidence to be a white boy. I hope you aren't just like the guys from my own race?"

"I guess we will have to see then." he told her and started undressing. He took off all of his clothes. He stood before her wearing his cowboy boots and his cowboy hat.

All Judy was looking at, was the baseball bat that was hanging in between his legs. She could not take her eyes off of it. It was as if it had her hypnotized. He saw that she was stuck and started walking towards her. As he walked his dick swung back and forth and her eyes followed it like a patient's eyes did when they were being hypnotized.

When he got in front of her he reached out and started unbuttoning her blouse. After he got her out of her blouse, he undid her pants. He pushed her back onto the bed and started removing her shoes. Once he got them off he pulled her pants and panties off. He climbed onto the bed and spread Judy's leg. Judy was locked in on his dick and she watched his as he guided it to her pussy's entrance. She had to see his dick go inside of her with her own eyes. She knew that a pussy stretched so that a baby could come out of it, but she did not know if it stretched just as much to let something come inside of it.

When Ted started pushing his dick into her, she started feeling as if she was about to be torn apart. She started trying to back up and every time that she would back up Ted would scoot up.

"Hold on there Missy, don't make me hog tie you." he told her. Once she was back against the headboard there was no place else for her to go. Ted put her legs on the sides of his waist and held her by her waist so that she couldn't move. He pulled her towards him as he pushed forward. He heard a loud pop then his dick was inside of her pussy.

Judy closed her eyes and tried to wish away the pain. She knew that he had ripped her down there, because she felt the liquid running down the inside of her legs. She thought to herself, "Yeah, he's in now, let's see what he is going to do. Just because he got an elephant's dick don't mean he knows how to use it."

She heard loud noises coming from the other room and wondered what she and Howdy Doody were doing over there. Tonya was in the other room being pounded. She could not believe it when Opie came out of his clothes and she saw that his dick hung down to the middle of his thighs. Once he was naked all of his shyness was gone. He had ordered Tonya to take her clothes off and once she was naked he had started ravishing her body. He did not get straight to the act like Ted. He began kissing Tonya in her mouth then he went to her breast. Next it was her pussy. He sucked her pussy like an expert. The combination of his tongue and fingers drove Tonya to two orgasms, before he had even started fucking her.

Ronnie had Tonya bend over the bed then he stood on top of the bed and mounted her like a horse mounted his mate. Tonya had never been fucked like that before. Ronnie even started making sounds like a horse as he fucked Tonya. Tonya loved it and she was glad that she had gone along with Judy's crazy idea. She would of never thought of fucking a white boy and wouldn't believe that there was one with a dick as big as his.

Ted sunk his dick all the way into Judy and just rocked inside of her for a few minutes. He wanted to give her pussy a few minutes to adjust to his dick before he started fucking her. When he pulled halfway out of her, he looked down and seen that there was a thin coat of blood on his dick. He knew that he had busted her out. He was ready to turn her pain into pleasure, and he started fucking her slowly. He had her legs cocked back in his arms as he fucked her.

He was going half out and half in for a while. When he heard her breathing become labored and soft moans start to escape her mouth he started going deeper and deeper with his strokes. Judy loved the way that he was dicking her. Waves of pleasure were going through her body. She started asking him for it.

"Give it to me you big dick white boy. Fuck me with your Garth Brooks looking ass."

"I'm going to break your achy breaky heart." he told her as he started pounding her.

Ronnie couldn't control himself inside of Tonya's pussy. He took both of his hands and twisted them inside of Tonya's hair, pulling her head back as he fucked her. He was fucking Tonya out of her mind and after he brought her to her third climax, she told him that she could not take it anymore. She wondered how was it that she had come three times and he hadn't come yet. She thought that she could suck his dick to get him to cum. She sat up on the end of the bed as he stood in front of her and sucked his dick.

Ted told Judy that it was time for her to do some bull riding and rolled over onto his back, while he was still inside of her. Judy started riding his dick. She put her hands flat on his stomach and started gyrating her hips in a circular motion.

"That's it ride the bull lady, hold on!" Ted told her as he started bucking and raising his hips up.

ŋ

Tonya felt as if she were getting lock jaw. Her jaws had become sore and Ronnie still hadn't cum.

"This shit is ridiculous!" she said to herself.

She asked Ronnie, "Have you taken a pill or something?"

"No, I don't do drugs it just takes a while for me to cum."

"Well, you have to give me a break I can't take it no more."

"That's okay I will go next door and see what they are doing." he told her. Ronnie walked over to the door opened it and entered the next room. He left the door open as he headed over to the bed. Judy heard the door open and turned her head to look behind her. "What the fuck!"

She could not believe what she saw. The white boy that looked like Harry Potter was standing next to the bed with a dick as big as Ted's.

"Where did they breed you guys at?"

"We are just good ole country boys." Ted told her.

"Why are you over here?" Ted asked Ronnie.

"Her friend said that she couldn't take anymore, so I have to join you two!" Ronnie told them as he got onto the bed. He positioned himself behind Judy and squatted down. Judy looked at the intent look on his face and the big dick that he was holding in his hand.

"What do you think your about to do?" Judy asked him.

"I'm about to rip your asshole out!" he told her as he took his dick and aimed it at her asshole.

"That thing is not going to fit in there."

"I'll get in in!" Ronnie told her as he went to spit in her asshole. Ted pulled Judy down to him, then took his hands and spread her ass cheeks for Ronnie. Ronnie pushed hard until the head of his dick popped in.

"Ow!" Judy screamed out.

Tonya heard Judy yell and walked over to the doorway. She looked into the room and seen Judy on top of Ted, while Ronnie was mounting her from the back. Ronnie put his hands onto her shoulders and pulled her to him as he pushed his dick all the way into her asshole. All three of them stayed in that position for a few minutes, and then Ronnie started moving. He started fucking Judy's ass slowly allowing her to get used to it. It was uncomfortable to her having a dick in her pussy and ass at the same time, but once she got adjusted she started moving. It wasn't long before they all were moving in sync. The feeling of pleasure was over powering for Judy.

She had never been fucked in both of her holes at the same time and to her the feeling was unbelievable. Even Tonya felt rejuvenated and couldn't wait to have her turn at getting fucked in her pussy and ass at the same time.

As soon as they were through with Judy, Tonya hopped onto the bed to have her turn. Judy just rolled over, staying on the bed to watch the action.

When Ronnie felt himself about to cum he told Tonya, "It's finally blast off time, brace yourself." He started blasting off in her asshole as Ted blasted off in her pussy.

After they were done, they all took turns taking a shower then got dressed. Before they left the room, they exchanged numbers and promised to meet up again. Judy and Tonya were in the car headed home, when Judy asked her, "So what do you think?"

"I guess there isn't anything wrong with having a little cream in our coffee."

Couldn't Tell The Difference

Tabitha and Tammy were identical twins and they had been close since they were kids. They grew up sharing everything from clothes to boys. As kids they would pull pranks on their boyfriends. They would dress alike and wear their hair in the same type of styles to fool their boyfriends.

One of them would be making out with their boyfriend, then make an excuse like they had to go to the bathroom. They would leave the room and the other twin would enter the room and resume making out with their boyfriend and he would never know the difference. That activity started as childhood games, but continued all the way into their adulthood.

In high school Tabitha had a boyfriend named Brian and he was about to be the one that she gave her virginity to. She told Tammy of her intentions and Tammy told her, "Wouldn't it be neat if he took both of our virginity on the same night?"

"And how do you propose that we do that?"

"After he pops your cherry, you tell him that you need to go and clean up. You leave out and I go in. He will think that he popped your cherry twice, until we show him different."

And that is what the twins did. Tabitha invited Brian over with the promise of letting him take her virginity. She assured him that her parents were not going to be home. Brian went to a separate high school from Tabitha and she never disclosed to him that she had a sister.

Brian came over late one Friday night and Tabitha took him into her bedroom. They did not waste any time. They got onto her twin bed and began kissing and grabbing all over each other. When Tabitha felt that it was time, she stood up and began removing her clothes, and Brian anxiously started to follow suite.

When they were both nude, Tabitha laid down on the bed and Brian crawled on top of her. He positioned himself between her legs and took one hand and guided his dick to her entrance. He had trouble lining his dick up with her hole, since her pussy was tightly closed. He licked one of his fingers and stuck it down between them. He located her pussy's entrance and pushed his finger in. Once he got one in, be put another one in.

He kept going until he had three of his fingers inside of her. Though they did not go deep, they still opened up her entrance enough for him to get the head of his dick in.

Once he got the head in, the pain shot through Tabitha. She put her arms around his back, closed her eyes and squeezed him as he pushed inside of her and popped her cherry. Once he was all the way in, her pussy was feeling tight it also felt cold and wet. He looked down and seen that his dick was coated with blood.

"You are bleeding!" he said to her.

"Let me go to the bathroom to clean up and get a towel, so that you can clean yourself up." Brian got up off of her and she got up and left the room. Brian walked over to the mirror and looked at himself, beaming with pride.

Tabitha was the first virgin that he had ever been with and he was basking in the glory.

After a few minutes, she reentered the room and handed him a towel, then laid back on the bed. After he cleaned himself off, he climbed back on top of her. He positioned his dick back at her entrance and found that he could not get back in. He fumbled around trying to get it in.

"What's wrong she asked?"

"I can't get it back in."

She raised her head and looked down, "The hot water must have caused me to close back up, open me up again." Brian went through the same process of getting his fingers inside of her again to get her open. Once he had her open enough, he put his dick back at her entrance and pushed   in.

They both heard a loud popping sound as his dick broke through her hymen. Brian thought to himself, "Damn! I took her virginity twice!" He looked down and seen that she was bleeding again.

"You're bleeding again!" he said to her.

"Let me go back to the bathroom right quick." Brian let her up and she left the room. He picked up the towel and cleaned himself off again. Tabitha came back into the room and Brian got back on top of her. This time it was a tight fit but his dick went all the way in. He did not have to bust through anything and there was no more blood.

"This is more like it." he said to Tabitha as he started fucking her. Tabitha started responding to him as the pain started to be replaced by pleasure. She raised her legs up and wrapped them around his waist, and then she put both of her hands on his ass and started pulling him deeper into her.

Brian loved the way that her pussy was feeling. Fucking a virgin's pussy was the best feeling in the world he thought to himself. All of a sudden he heard the bedroom door open and looked up. He saw a girl who looked exactly like Tabitha walking naked towards the bed. Brian stopped in mid stroke and kept looking from one Tabitha to the other one.

He thought that his mind was playing tricks on him. He closed his eyes, shook his head back and forth then opened his eyes. One Tabitha was still under him and the other one was standing right next to the bed.

Brian rolled off of Tabitha onto his back, while the other Tabitha climbed onto the bed.

"What's going on?" he asked confused, looking from one Tabitha to the other.

"That is my twin sister Tammy and today, you popped both of our cherries." Brian could not believe what he was seeing or what he was hearing.

"So I had sex with both of you two?"

"That's right and you are not finished, I need my turn." Tammy said to him as she laid on her back and began to spread her legs. Brian looked to Tabitha, who told him, "Go ahead and finish what you started." Brian's dick instantly sprang back to life and he climbed between Tammy's legs. He sunk his dick all the way into her then began fucking her. He decided that he wanted to fuck her in a different position from the one that he had fucked her sister, so he had her get into the doggy style position and fucked her from behind. When Tabitha got doggy style next to her sister she turned to him, "See if you can tell us apart by our pussies."

Brian started going back and forth fucking the sisters from behind. To him their pussy felt exactly the same. He could not tell the twins apart from looking at their face or fucking their pussies. He enjoyed the way that both of their pussies were feeling.

Tabitha got up from her position, while he was fucking Tammy. He put all of his concentration into fucking Tammy and all of a sudden he felt something wet on his balls. He thought that maybe she had started bleeding again and looked down to check. He was shocked to see Tabitha sucking on his balls. Just the sight of her sucking his balls made him blast off inside of Tammy.

After they were finished, they all got dressed. The twins told Brian that if he promised to keep what happened between them a secret, that they could continue to have threesomes together, Brian told them, "My lips are sealed." he left headed home thinking to himself, "Who would even believe that I went from never having popped a cherry, to popping two in one day, twins at that?" He whistled the rest of his way home.

He Liked To Watch

Harry grabbed the bag that contained his bowling ball, grabbed his bowling shoes and headed downstairs. Suanne was sitting on the couch and he told her, "I'm off to the bowling alley honey. I won't be home until around midnight, so you don't have to wait up for me." Suanne gave Harry a sad look.

"You always stay out so late dear."

"Suanne, you know that Thursday is men's night out. We bowl and afterwards we go out to have drinks and just lollygag."

"I know honey, you have a good time." she said to him then got up and gave him a hug and a kiss. Harry left out of the house, got into his car and pulled out of the driveway.

Suanne stood at the window with the curtains slightly pulled back and watched Harry drive off. As soon as he turned the corner she ran over to the couch, grabbed her cell phone from under the cushion and called Greg. He answered his phone and Suanne told him, "He's gone, come on over, we have four hours to have fun."

"I'm on my way!" Greg told her then hung up the phone. Suanne ran around the house, anxiously preparing for Greg's arrival.

Harry had only driven around the corner and parked his car. He sat there thinking about how it all began. One morning, when Suanne was standing at the bus stop waiting to catch the bus to work, Greg had appeared. For a week straight they caught the bus from the same bus stop. He told Suanne that his car was in the shop getting repaired, so he was going to be catching the bus to work for a week. They would chat every morning while they waited on the bus. The first day Suanne felt uncomfortable talking to Greg, who was black. She had never really associated with black men before, and Greg was a little intimidating, standing at 6' 3" and weighing about two hundred and sixty pounds.

By the second day, she started taking in how Greg had a nice easy going personality. He actually made her feel comfortable and the way that he talked to her was as if they had known each other for a while.

On the third day, Greg was giving her comments telling her how pretty she was and how her husband was lucky to have her. He told her that he always fantasized about being with someone from a different race, but had never came across the opportunity.

Suanne started thinking, "Harry doesn't realize how lucky he is. He never spends time with me anymore and our sex life is starting to be pathetic." She took in the fact that Greg was handsome. She had never been attracted to black men before, but the more that she looked at Greg the more attracted to him she became. She stood there wondering what it would be like having sex with a black man. She had heard the stories about how black men were supposed to be hung like horses. She sneaked a peak down to his crotch area as he was talking, trying to see his dick print. He had on dress slacks and she did not see anything.

"It's probably just a myth." she said to herself. The bus came and they got on. Greg took a seat next to Suanne and they continued having a conversation until Suanne reached her stop.

That night at home, Harry sat there telling her how he couldn't wait to get with the fellas the next night, for their weekly bowling tournament. To Suanne, Harry was becoming more and more boring. He never did anything fun and exciting with her anymore, it was always him and his friends. Suanne tried to initiate sex with him that night and all of a sudden he was tired and needed to get some sleep to get prepared for the big day the next day.

After Harry had gone to bed, Suanne laid on the living room couch. She closed her eyes and Greg's face popped up in her head. Suanne found herself becoming aroused. She pulled her skirt up, pulled her panties to the side and slid two of her fingers inside of her pussy. Her pussy became super wet as she visualized Greg fucking her. She used her two fingers to finger fuck herself to an orgasm. She came and fell asleep right there on the couch.

The next morning, she got up, took a shower, and then got ready for work. She left the house and headed to the bus stop. When she got there, Greg was already there and she blushed as thoughts from the night before entered her mind. Greg took notice and said to her, "You must of had a good night?"

"Yes, it was okay, I guess."

"I had a horrible night. It was just me and a TV dinner. I sure could go for a home cooked meal." Suanne's mind started turning. She knew that Harry was going to his bowling tournament, so she decided to offer Greg a home cooked meal.

"Are you busy tonight?" she asked him.

"No why?"

"Well, I am cooking tonight. Maybe you could come by and have a plate?"

"Your husband wouldn't mind?"

"Harry could care less, besides he is not going to be there."

"I don't want to be any trouble, if it's not going to put you out there or anything?"

"No! No! Everything is fine." she assured him. Their bus came, they got on it and Greg sat next to her. She asked him for his phone number and told him that she would call and tell him what time to come over and give him the address.

When Suanne got home from work she was in a good mood as she went into the kitchen and started preparing dinner. Harry noticed her mood.

"You got some good news dear?"

"Why do you ask that?"

"You just seem so happy."

"There is nothing wrong with me being happy is it?"

"No darling, but you do know that I will be eating out with the fellas tonight."

"Yes I know I'm going to put your plate up."

"Okay!" Harry told her then went upstairs to get ready. After he was ready he went downstairs with his bowling gear, gave Suanne a kiss then headed out of the door. Soon as he was gone, she called Greg, gave him the address and told him to come on over. After she hung up from him, Suanne set the table, made sure that the food was ready, then went and took a shower.

When she got out of the shower, she put on some scented perfume all over her body. She put on the shortest skirt that she could find, without putting any underwear on, and started applying makeup.

Twenty minutes later she heard the doorbell ring and went to answer it. She opened the door and there stood Greg wearing a sweater and a pair of jeans. Suanne invited him in, and escorted him into the kitchen. She told him, "Have a seat I'm going to grab the roast out of the oven. Greg took a seat and Suanne went over to the stove. She put on a pair of mittens then opened up the oven. When she bent over to pull out the roast, Greg seen that she wasn't wearing any panties. Suanne's big, meaty, pink pussy lips were sticking out from between her thighs.

Greg knew then that he was about to get his first piece of white ass. His dick got so hard that he thought that there wasn't enough room in his pants for him to sit comfortably. He slid his chair up to the table, unzipped his pants and pulled his dick out. He breathed a sigh of relief as his dick broke free.

When Suanne stood up, Greg told her, "Your roast looks lovely."

"Why thank you." Suanne said to him thinking that he was talking about the roast that she held in her hands. In actuality he was talking about her ass.

Suanne set the rest of the food onto the table and they ate. Once they were finished with the main course, Greg said, "That was the best meal that I have had in a long time. I can't wait to taste your dessert." Suanne did not catch what he meant and frowned, because she became mad at herself. She was so concerned about making the perfect dinner that she had forgotten all about making any dessert.

"Greg, I am so sorry, but I was so caught up with making dinner that I did not even make any dessert."

"Do you have any whip cream?" Confused by his question, Suanne responded, "I think that there is some in the cabinet."

"Okay, you grab that and I will make my own dessert." Suanne went over to the cabinet, opened it and up on the top shelf sat the whip cream. She had to get up on her tip toes to reach it, and her skirt rose up to the middle of her ass cheeks when she reached up. Suanne felt the cold air on her ass and quickly tried to reach behind her with one hand to pull the skirt down. She felt a hand on her ass. Greg was standing behind her so close, that she could smell his scent.

"There is no need to cover up." he said to her as he reached up and grabbed the whip cream.

"I need it up so that I can make my dessert." He grabbed Suanne's hand and led her out to the living room. He had her pull her skirt up to her waist and sit on the couch. He had her pull her legs bent at the knees, up onto the couch, and then he got on his knees. He shook the can of whip cream removed the top and began spraying it on her pussy. The cool sensation sent a shiver through Suanne's body. Greg lowered his head and started licking the cream off of her pussy.   Suanne started going crazy as he lapped the cream off of her pussy.

Things really got crazy when Greg told her to get up and turn around. He had Suanne on her knees bent over the back of the couch. He had her spread her ass cheeks apart, while he sprayed whip cream on her pussy and asshole. Greg went to eating her pussy and ass. Suanne lost all control and started saying things that she had never said before.

"Eat it mother fucker."

"You nasty fucker you eating my shit hole,"

"Fuck! it feels so good." After all the cream was gone and Suanne had reached two orgasms, Greg stood up and started removing his clothes. He took off every stitch of clothing that he had on. Suanne was in the same position, looking back over her shoulder at him. When she seen his dick she almost fell out.

"My God it is true you are hung like a horse." She quickly turned around and sat down.

"You have to let me suck it." Greg stood in front of her and told her, "Like Burger King have it your way!" Suanne reached out and grabbed his dick with both of her hands. She used both of them to try and measure its length. She found that she needed four hands. She realized that she was slobbing as she looked at his dick and lowered her mouth onto it.

She slobbered all over his dick as Greg stood in front of her with his hands on his hips and legs spread. Suanne used her hands and cupped his balls. She fondled them and rubbed them as she sucked him off.

"Yes Suanne!"

"Oh yes!"

"You suck the hell out of a dick."

"Take it in baby put it in the back of your throat." Suanne tried to take him all the way in and started to gag. She had to back up off of it some.

Harry was outside of the window watching. He saw his wife acting like an animal. She was sucking Greg's dick like it was the only one on the planet and that it was going to be her only chance at getting it. That wasn't it, things got better when Greg told

Suanne, "It's time now that I get some of that rump roast." He had Suanne get onto the floor into the doggy style position and mounted her. He put his dick into Suanne and she went crazy.

"You black mother fucker, where have you been all my life? You make me feel so full." Harry watched through the window as Suanne went crazy, shaking her head from side to side and talking real dirty. He had never heard her talk dirty like that. He pulled his dick out and began jacking off as he watched Greg pound his wife. Harry couldn't contain himself after he heard Suanne tell Greg, "Put in my ass!" He had been with his wife for over fourteen years and she had never offered him her shit hole. Harry came as hard as he watched Greg ass fuck his wife that he shot his nut all over their window.

Greg told Suanne, "I'm about to fill you up!" then he skeeted in her asshole. Suanne was so tired that she fell face down onto the floor and laid there, even after Greg was gone. She was still lying on the floor, when she heard keys in the door.

"Oh shit!" she said and quickly jumped up, grabbed her things and headed into the bedroom. She did not even have time to get dressed, so she threw her things under the bed and jumped under the covers asshole naked.

Harry came into the room as if everything was normal. He took off all of his clothes and climbed into the bed with Suanne, who was playing   sleep. He eased up behind her, "Oh dear, you must have been waiting on me." he whispered in her ear.

He slid his finger into her pussy and she acted as if she was just now coming awake.

"You're home?"

"Yes dear and your pussy is so wet."

"I was dreaming about you."

"I can tell!" Harry told her as he slid his dick into her. Harry started fucking her like he had never done before. The way that he was fucking her, turned her on and she started fucking him back. Harry had not fucked her like he was doing in a long time. She was wondering what had gotten into him. Whatever it was, she loved it.

Harry knew that she was none the wiser, that he had sent Greg at her. Greg was a guy that he had met at a bar and developed a relationship with. Harry had confided   in Greg that he had fantasies about watching his wife get fucked by a black man. He asked Greg if he would be interested. At first Greg thought Harry was loony, and then he realized that all types of people had sick, twisted fantasies. He decided that if Harry wanted to watch his wife get fucked by a black guy, then he would give his service.

Harry had told him things about Suanne that he would know would get her to lighten up. He told him where she caught the bus to and from work and Greg had taken it from there.

It was planned that every Thursday night, Harry would act like he was leaving to go bowling and would come back and watch the action. That had been two months ago. This night when Harry left like he was going bowling, he had intentions of sneaking back into the house and busting Suanne. He felt that it was time for the charade to be over and it was time to bring everything out into the open. Greg knew what was going to happen and just played his part.

When he got there Suanne opened the door completely naked and as soon as he was inside she closed the door and began snatching off his clothes. She dropped to her knees and started sucking his dick right by the front door. She had fallen in love with sucking Greg's dick. She loved everything about it, the length, the width and the taste.

Greg knew that Harry was due to bust in at any minute, so he pulled Suanne up and led her over by the couch. He had her get back on her knees, with her back to the door and she started sucking his dick again. Her hair hung down in front of her face and she never heard the front door open. Harry stepped inside, quietly closed the door and began stripping his clothes off. When he was naked, he eased over to his wife and kneeled behind her. Greg reached behind Suanne to spread her ass cheeks, while Harry guided his dick into her. Suanne's eyes flew open from shock and she turned her head. She said, "Harry!" then fainted.

She collapsed to the floor and Harry rolled her over onto her back. Greg ran into the kitchen grabbed a cup of cold water and took it back to Harry. Harry poured some of the cold water onto Suanne's face. Water got into her nose and she came to coughing and choking. She opened her eyes and found that she was face to face with Harry. She looked around the room and seen Greg standing nearby still nude. She had no idea as to what was going on or what to say. Harry did it for her, "It's okay Suanne. This was all set up by me." Suanne just looked at Harry trying to figure out what he was talking about.

"I always had fantasies of watching you fuck another man. Really a black man and I did not think that you would go for it if I asked you, so I sent Greg at you."

"You have been watching us have sex for over two months!"

"You set all of this up?"

"You are sick Harry!"

"Suanne, let's not go pointing fingers and throwing out titles, you haven't exactly been an angel."

"You sure have been liking what you have been getting."

"You have been calling ole Greg faithfully so you have been getting what you wanted and I have been getting what I wanted. Now I feel it's time for both of us to stop doing it secretly and just be out in the open with each other."

"You want me to have sex with another man while you watch Harry?"

"You have been doing it unknowingly anyway, so there shouldn't be a problem." he turned to Greg.

"Greg, do finish having your way with my wife." Greg approached Suanne.

"Come on baby, it's not that bad. You will forget that he's even here once I get this dick in you." Suanne looked down and seen that Greg's dick had sprang to life. She was hooked on it and could not turn it down. Greg laid her on the floor, while Harry took a seat in the end chair. Suanne laid on the floor on her back with tears running down her eyes as Greg got between her legs and put his dick inside of her. Suanne turned her head and looked at Harry, who sat looking expressionless at them.

Greg started fucking Suanne like they were the only ones in the room and after a while Suanne started feeling the same way. She forgot that Harry was even there, as she began spread her legs out wide, grabbed her ankles and held them. She could not even keep her mouth closed "Yes Greg, fuck me dear, bang this white pussy.

Put that black dick in me!" Greg started fucking the shit out of Suanne and Harry started jacking his dick. When he felt like he was about to cum, he went and stood over Suanne and busted off on her face. He went and sat back in the chair and finished watching the show. After Greg came, Harry told him that he would see him next Thursday.

Suanne got up and was about to go take a shower, but Harry told her, "Come back here!" He put her on the floor doggy style and began fucking the shit out of her. Now Suanne understood how every Thursday he would fuck her royally. Watching her get fucked by another man turned him on, to the point that he would come home and fuck the shit out of her. After it was all out in the open, they kept up the routine with Greg for many years.

Bonus: Just Nasty

Janae was drunk and wanted to get fucked. She called Jamal to see if she could get a booty call. Jamal, who was just leaving the club with his boys, answered his phone, "What's up?"

"Jamal, this is Janae, where are you at?" Jamal could tell that Janae was drunk and his dick got hard knowing that she wanted to fuck. He instantly regretted that he had agreed to drive his boys to the club in his Excursion. He had four of his friends with him and was going to have to drop them off at three different locations before he could head over to Janae's house.

"I'm just leaving the club why?" he responded to her question.

"I'm drunk and want to get fucked."

"I got to drop my boys off then I'm on my way."

"I ain't trying to wait that long bring them with you." Jamal got hyped, thinking that she was thirsty for his dick. He covered the phone and told his boys, "Y'all got to roll with me, while I shoot over to Janae's house." They all got to mumbling, but he did not care. He decided that he wasn't   going to miss a chance at getting some of her good head.

He uncovered the phone and told Janae, "I'm on my way!" Then he hung up.

Janae was sitting in her living room drinking Jack Daniels and watching a porno on her satellite television. She thought to herself, "I got a surprise for them, when they get over here. Tonight, I feel like being fucked by more than one man, and his boys that he have with him, they all can get it."

Jamal sped over to Janae's house, with Monk, Smitty, Paul and Pookie all in his truck.

"Man that bitch better have some friends over there!" Pookie spoke out saying.

"Yeah, we ain't going to be sitting up in no living room, while you up in her bedroom getting some ass!" Monk jumped in saying. Jamal wasn't paying his boys any mind. All he was thinking about was getting up in Janae's super tight pussy.

When he pulled in front of Janae's house, he cut off his truck, took the keys out of the ignition, and then jumped out of the truck. All of his friends climbed out of the truck after him and followed him up to the door. Jamal knocked on the door and Janae opened it.

After she opened the door, she turned and walked away. Jamal was shocked that she only had on a small t-shirt with no underwear on. He thought she was going to head straight to her bedroom, and decided that he was going to try to hold his boys up until she got out of sight. Paul, who was much taller than him looked over his shoulder and saw Janae's bare ass cheeks. He pushed past Jamal saying, "Damn!"

The rest of the fellas wanted to see what was going on and started pushing into the house also.

Janae went back over to the couch and flopped down on it. She pulled her legs up onto the couch, which made the t-shirt rise up and her pussy was put on display. They all stood next to each other staring at her pussy.

Janae told Pookie who was closes to the door, "Close my door and lock it." Pookie did as he was told. Then they all looked at Jamal dumbfounded. He was just as shocked as them and did not know how to take what Janae was doing. They all stood there with hard dicks staring at Janae. They all felt that she could get it. She only stood 5' 3" and was a little overweight, but she had some big titties and a fat ass. They were waiting on Jamal to make a move.

Janae put two fingers into her pussy and began finger fucking herself and Jamal couldn't take it anymore. He had to find out what was going on.

"Janae, what's up?" he asked her.

"Shit I'm waiting on you scary mother fuckers to make a move. I'm drunk, I feel freaky, and I want to be treated like a slut by all of you. How many is it?" she asked then started counting them with her hands.

"It's five of you and y'all are all standing up there scared to death of this pussy, got me playing in it myself."

"We can all get it?" Pookie asked as he headed towards her.

"If y'all can handle it then y'all can get it."

"Say no more!" Pookie told her as he unzipped his pants and pulled his dick out. He approached Janae with his dick in his hand and she looked at it.

"It's nice but I've seen bigger!" she told him as she reached out, grabbed it and pulled him to her. She put his dick in her mouth and started sucking it. Paul shot over to the couch and kneeled down in front of her and replaced her fingers with his and started finger fucking her.

"Damn your pussy is super wet!" he said to her. All Janae could do was moan on Pookie's dick. Monk rushed over to the couch he pulled his dick out and Janae reached out and grabbed it. She started dry jacking it.

Smitty said, "Y'all got to do better than that, so we can all get on, let her get in a better position." Pookie pulled his dick out of her mouth and she got doggy style on the couch, facing the side of it. Paul got on the couch behind her and put his dick in her, fucking her doggy style, while Pookie went around to the side of the couch and put his dick back into her mouth. Janae greedily sucked his dick, while Paul fucked her. Those two had their way with her, and then they tagged the other two in. Monk got her from the back and Smitty went to the front and pulled his dick out.

"Now that is what I have been looking for." Janae said then put his dick into her mouth. She jacked and sucked Smitty's dick at the same time and when he started to cum she pulled his dick out of her mouth and let him cum all over her face. She milked all of his cum out onto her face. When she was finished with his dick, she looked around and asked, "Where is Jamal at?" Everyone looked around the room and saw no sign of him.

"Fuck him, his dick ain't shit anyway, I want all of y'all at one time." Janae got off of the couch and got down onto the floor. She laid on her back to spread her legs. Pookie climbed in between them and started fucking her. Paul knelt down in front of her face and put his dick into her mouth. Smitty and Monk both knelt down on the sides of her and she began jacking them off. They all had their way with Janae.

They fucked her in the ass and skeeted on her face and breast. When they were through, Janae told them to get dressed and leave. They were all mad at Jamal for leaving them, causing them to have to walk home.

Janae locked the door behind them, then went into the bathroom and looked at herself in the mirror. She had their cum all over her face and breast. She licked some from the corners of her mouth and said to herself, "That's just nasty!"

New Flavor Books & Publishing LLC
Book Order form

Full Name: _____

Institution# (If applicable):_____

Address: _____

Address 2: _____

City:_____ State:_____ Zip:_____

Book Title:	Price/Quantity
Hood to Hood: A Cleveland Story	$15.99 ____
Hood to Hood 2: Spank's Revenge	$15.99 ____
Sexual Addiction: Director's cut	$15.99 ____
All Flavors A book of Erotic Short Stories	$9.99 ____
Bisexual Bliss	$15.99 ____
Murder or Justice	$15.99 ____
Hittin' Licks	$15.99 ____
Deadly Surgeon	$15.99____

Total Including ($3.00) Shipping and Handling _____

To place an order for one of our books please send a payment
for the price of the book plus $3.00 for shipping and handling to:
New Flavor Books & Publishing LLC
C/O Book orders
PO Box 603323
Cleveland, Ohio 44103
Please allow 2 - 4 weeks

www.ingramcontent.com/pod-product-compliance
Lightning Source LLC
Chambersburg PA
CBHW051846170626
46807CB00003B/1371